A Leap of *Faith*

An accomplished dream

Monica Raghavan

ISBN
Paperback 979-8-89026-429-9
Hardcase 979-8-89026-759-7

Acknowledgements

Having an idea and turning it into a book is as hard as it sounds. The experience is both internally challenging and rewarding.

My heartfelt appreciation goes to my extremely supportive husband Vikram, and my two adorable children Aryaan and Advika who are my immense source of joy and happiness. I am eternally grateful to my parents who taught me discipline, responsibilities, honesty and compassion and so much more that has helped me succeed. I am thankful to my in-laws for their consistent love and to the rest of my family.

Thanks to my darling sister Nivedita for being my critic and inspiration at every step. None of this would have been possible without the support of my brother and my dearest aunt who has always been there for me.

I want to express my deep appreciation to T. K. Vineeth for his keen insight and valuable support. A very special thanks to Vineet K. Silaniya and Anubhuti for motivating me, and my dear friends who have always encouraged me.

My deepest gratitude to my mentor, Dr Daisaku Ikeda, philosopher, educator and author whose constant guidance and inspiration have been like a compass that has steered me through all of my endeavours.

I thank the entire Notion Press team for their constant support.

And last, but certainly not the least, you, the reader. Your consistent affection, understanding and encouragement are what I deeply cherish. Thank you so much. God bless all of you.

Contents

Acknowledgements   *3*

Chapter 1   The Daily Humdrum   7

Chapter 2   Sisters   12

Chapter 3   Special Moments   16

Chapter 4   Fate's Game   22

Chapter 5   Breakdown   26

Chapter 6   The Briefcase   31

Chapter 7   Building Moments of Strength   34

Chapter 8   A Stranger's Note   37

Chapter 9   Crossroads   40

Chapter 10   New Beginnings   44

Chapter 11   The Journey Begins   49

Chapter 12   The Weavers' Hub   54

Chapter 13   A Close Encounter   60

Chapter 14   A Success Story   71

Chapter 15   Shadows from the Past   78

Chapter 16   Monsoon Season in Mumbai   87

Chapter 17   The Quest   94

Chapter 1
The Daily Humdrum

The gentle rays of the morning sun filtered through the slightly drawn curtains of the window in the bedroom. Shirin's sun-kissed face glowed as she woke up and groggily walked into the kitchen to prepare her favourite Darjeeling tea. The wooden jar of aromatic leaves reminded her of the memorable trip to the foothills of the Eastern Himalayas with Arjun, her husband, and her two adorable daughters, Kamini and Kiara. It had just been a month since they returned from an exciting, fun-filled trip they had been looking forward to for a long time. They were a happy family who loved travelling to quaint places, especially when they needed to escape from the daily humdrum of life.

Shirin sipped her tea as she relaxed on a reclining chair and immersed herself in thoughts of her college days. The jasmine flower's lovely scent filled the air as she inhaled deeply. Shirin had always been an independent working woman who worked as a fashion designer for a well-known apparel company. She took a break from her promising career after having her first child, Kamini.

But Shirin had no regrets for the decision or any other decision she made in her life, for that matter. She was a free spirit and had a carefree attitude, always brimming with life. Her lovely silky black hair like the night sky covered her beautiful round hip. Shirin appeared more attractive because of the dimple on her chin and the broadness of her pointed nose which were the highlights of her brown skin tone.

She was barely twenty-five when she decided to marry Arjun, the love of her life. Arjun was 6 foot tall, a strapping young man with sharply chiselled features and light brown eyes. He had a faint scar near his right cheek. During his teenage years, when he was learning to ride a bicycle, Arjun fell off and hit his face on a stone, which gave him a scar. Arjun was highly ambitious. He had a flourishing family business in garments and was the leading manufacturer of a well-known brand in the garment industry. He wanted to expand his business globally and had been offered a great opportunity by a leading international brand to manufacture clothes for their market in South America.

Shirin had met Arjun in the first year of her college. His parents had always wanted him to marry a girl with an influential background and solid financial backing, who would perfectly integrate into their a-la-posh hoity-toity society. They always wanted him to marry a fair, tall, and slender girl whom they could proudly introduce to the glitzy and wealthy people of Tinseltown. But Shirin was a complete contrast to their expectations. Shirin hailed from a middle-class family and was proud of her dusky beauty. She was aware of Arjun's attraction to her wit and exuberance, her character's strengths.

Shirin had met Arjun for the first time at the university canteen. It was love at first sight for Arjun. He knew she was the girl of his dreams and the love of his life. He also knew that his parents would never approve of their marriage because of the vast difference in their family backgrounds. Shirin's father was a university professor, while her mother was a nurse in a government hospital. Despite Arjun's parents' disapproval, they eventually got married.

Shirin's life had changed completely after marriage. She wasn't acquainted with the other side of Arjun and gradually discovered it a few months after their wedding. Arjun was a domineering husband who would not let Shirin make independent decisions. He would be the one to make all significant choices for the household. For the sake of domestic tranquillity, Shirin avoided arguing with Arjun.

Shirin was sipping her early morning cup of tea on her balcony, still lost in thought. The aroma of Darjeeling tea reminded her of the summer trip to the famed hill station. She had been planning a trip with her family for a while. Arjun would not have readily accepted the vacation because he was preoccupied with his business. Shirin desired a relaxing trip to the hills with the kids. She always admired the tranquillity and the beauty of the hills. Arjun needed to be prodded and persuaded to go on the trip. He had no choice but to agree to the Darjeeling trip since Kiara and Kamini were adamant about going there. Shirin grinned and expressed her gratitude for the opportunity to travel to Darjeeling as a family during the summer break with Arjun and the kids. The family had a wonderful time together in the picturesque beauty of the Eastern Himalayas. A few days had passed, and Shirin had observed Arjun's constant expression of worry ever since the family returned from their trip to Darjeeling.

'I must find out what Arjun has been thinking about,' she decided.

Shirin was distracted by the commotion of the birds on the neem tree outside her balcony. It was time to wake up everyone in the house. So, she glanced at the time. Shirin's phone's alarm went off just as she was about to enter the kid's room. It was 6:30 a.m., and she rushed to wake up the kids to avoid them getting late to school.

She dashed into the children's bedroom and, in a sweet tone, said, "Upsy-Daisy, my sleepy little heads."

Little Kiara had turned ten just a week ago.

She rubbed her eyes and said, "Mamma, why does the sun pop out so early in the morning?"

Shirin said with a warm smile, "To wake up our darling Kiara."

Shirin called out her elder daughter, Kamini. "Kamini, it's 6:45 in the morning. Aren't you getting late for school, my darling? I remember you saying last night that a special announcement would be made in school today."

Kamini jumped out of bed since it was her special day in school. She was a robust fourteen-year-old teenager who knew the art of pushing through things. She was stubborn and independent in her thoughts. Today, senior secondary students' inter-school basketball competition results were to be announced.

"I am sure our school will bag the award this time. Bingo!" said Kamini.

Kamini and Kiara were so different from each other as siblings. Kamini was strong-headed, while Kiara was gentle and obedient, always ready to take instructions from her mom.

Shirin went to her room to see if Arjun was dressed for the office. She noticed he had forgotten to button up all the shirt buttons.

Shirin said, "Look, you haven't buttoned up your shirt properly. I have noticed something has been bothering you since we returned from the trip. Tell me all about it, Arjun."

But her husband seemed oblivious to the fact that Shirin was talking to him and did not pay much heed to what she said. She found his behaviour strange and it dawned upon her that Arjun wasn't himself anymore. He used to greet Shirin in the morning by kissing her forehead; she expected the same today. Shirin was alarmed but put on a forced smile and came a few steps closer to him, but her partner was obviously upset about something but didn't try to hide it while trying to rummage through his wardrobe drawer.

"I don't know, Shirin, why do you have to touch my things? Did you see a small black briefcase?" Arjun yelled at his wife, knitting his eyebrows to produce an irritated look. He clicked his tongue and added, "I wonder where the briefcase vanished?"

Shirin was taking out her clothes from the wardrobe.

"You can't blame me every time for things getting misplaced in the house," Shirin said with an irritated expression.

She bent down to pick up Arjun's socks from the floor. "I am the one who keeps the house clean and tidy." But before she could say anything further, he hurriedly left the room as he was getting late for work.

Shirin was thinking of ways to find out the reason for what had been upsetting Arjun. Shirin thought of making his favourite kheer with jaggery to change his mood.

Chapter 2
Sisters

Shirin's family resided in a charming, quiet neighbourhood, away from the bustling crowd. They had moved into the lovely home with a lush green expanse just two years prior. After her father's death, Shirin was utterly heartbroken and was trying to accept that nothing is eternal. All our loved ones leave behind the lovely memories we share when they pass away.

From the large hallway to the open door, the house exuded warmth. The cosy, comforting rooms had a personal touch, all furnished by Shirin herself. She yearned for a life free from the humdrum of the bustling metropolis. After everyone had left, the house was empty, and Shirin was ready to brew her next cup of tea. This was her time to relax and spend a quiet, pensive moment with herself. She leaned back on her rocking chair with a cup of tea on her flower-dotted green balcony.

Shirin was thinking about Arjun's sudden change of behaviour and absent-mindedness when her mobile suddenly rang. It was Roshani Didi calling her.

"Hello, Didi. I haven't heard from you for a long time," said Shirin as she sprung up and repositioned herself on the rocking chair.

"I want you to come shopping with me over the weekend," said Roshani.

Shirin reluctantly said, "But I have to go for an important social commitment. Can we do it next weekend?"

"You always have excuses to make, Shirin, whenever I have important work. You can do your work some other day. Come along with me and I will not accept any excuses this time," said Roshani.

Shirin couldn't say no to her elder sister Roshani. She always looked up to her and had a lot of respect for her elder sister. Roshani was tall and slender, with beautiful cheekbones and delicate physical features. She was the apple of her parent's eyes, thoroughly spoiled and pampered. Shirin always felt that she was constantly compared with her sister; Roshani was academically inclined and always topped her class, while Shirin was average in her studies. Shirin's parents' expectations of her were pretty high. They wanted her to do well in school and ace her class. A constant comparison between the two sisters left Roshani feeling superior to her sister in many ways. Shirin always underestimated herself, thinking Roshani was more qualified and smarter than her. Roshani was popular among the boys and was known in school as the girl who had beauty with brains. This led Shirin to harbour a lot of doubts about herself.

As the years passed, Roshani studied and qualified with a PhD in physics. She never wanted to be a part of the corporate world and chose not to work after marriage. Her husband, Raman, was her school friend. Being the son of an industrialist, he was super rich and was born with a silver spoon. Raman had been madly in love with Roshani since they were in tenth grade. Raman always wanted to marry Roshani and was never attracted to other girls. Even though many girls tried to win his heart, it was Roshani who stole his heart. They were both destined to be together and were made for each other.

Shirin always admired her elder sister and wished she had all her qualities. Her parents' constant comparison with Roshani led to Shirin's gradual simmering of envy and jealousy towards her sister and she often battled with this thought and brushed it aside with guilt. She recalled an incident when Roshani was in college and smiled upon remembering it. It was Roshani's twentieth birthday. Raman had planned a surprise birthday party for Roshani. Raman had told Shirin to get Roshani to the Bistro pub, the most popular pub in town, without letting her know since this was a surprise birthday party.

Roshani had asked, "Where is Raman? He was supposed to meet me at the café. I wonder why you are taking me to the most expensive pub in the city."

When Roshani entered the pub, loud head-banging music was blaring. It annoyed Roshani greatly, and she was ready to stream out. Suddenly, the music stopped, and a birthday song started to play. Raman looked handsome in a blue T-shirt and baggy jeans and smiled lopsidedly. Roshani was over the moon and full of excitement. She blushed and smiled at Raman. Shirin saw the romantic couple and wished in her heart that someday she would also find her true love. Roshani was ecstatic to know that Raman had organised this to make her birthday special. Raman proposed to Roshani that day. Shirin's parents were delighted that their daughter would be married into an affluent family.

We all yearn for pure love.

Love that will warm the cockles of our hearts.

It is love that will see us through these dark times.

Love that will warm our hearts even on a cold winter day.

Love in its purest form is like the bright, golden sun.

It will warm our hearts even on a chilly winter day.

That illuminates everything it passes through.

Roshani and Raman finally married, and Roshani's parents were the happiest. Shirin wished to have a fairy tale wedding like Roshani Didi someday.

Chapter 3
Special Moments

Rays of sunlight lit up the children's room as Kamini hurled open the curtains. With all the activity in the room, little Kiara was tossing and turning on her warm and cosy bed.

"Wake up, sleepy head," said Kamini. "Today is a special day. It's Mamma's birthday."

Little Kiara stirred in her bed and tried to open her sleepy eyes. It was a bright April morning, and it seemed to Kiara as if the sunbeams were knocking on the window pane, waiting to be let in. It was a lazy Sunday morning, and when Kamini looked at the watch, it was 8 a.m.

"How can you wake me up so early on a holiday? I am going back to sleep," said Kiara with a frown.

Kamini gave a stern look to her baby sister and said, "Alright, I will take all the credit for preparing a perfect Sunday breakfast for Mama, my lazy sleeping beauty."

Kamini walked out of the room. Kiara groggily followed her sister to the kitchen. Kamini and Kiara were all excited to make a special breakfast for Shirin. Kamini knew Mamma's favourite breakfast was toast with garlic butter and cheese omelette topped with fresh herbs from the garden, especially parsley and fresh orange juice in a tall glass. Kiara suggested to Kamini that they could make a smiley face for Mama with honey on the toast.

"Great idea!" said Kamini. "Let's just do that. It would be fun!"

Kamini googled to see what special cheese omelette she could make, and yes, she found the perfect easy recipe. Well, it would not be served plain. The food had to be plated with a bouquet in a vase and a well-decorated floral napkin on a tray.

Little Kiara jumped and said, "I will carry the flowers while you carry the tray with all the food. Mamma will be so happy and will feel very special."

Kamini sneered at Kiara and teasingly said, "Well! In that case, Mamma would receive only an empty tray because you would have dropped all the food on the floor and scattered all the decorations by the time we get to Mamma's bedroom." Kamini laughed uncontrollably.

Kiara scorned at her sister's comments and just pretended to ignore her. Kamini and Kiara glided up to their parent's bedroom with bouncy steps, all excited to see their mother's reaction. The kids knew that Shirin always loved having breakfast in the garden. She always looked forward to the garden breakfast season that would start in mid-October when there would be a slight nip in the air, and the sun was warm and mellow. Shirin would love to sit in the garden after having a nice head bath, letting her beautiful cascading hair fall to her waist. There was a symbiosis between Shirin and the beautiful garden she painstakingly laboured over, particularly in the spring when the flowers were budding and the sweet-smelling fragrances of the flowers mixed in the air. The girls tiptoed into their parents' bedroom and saw Shirin slowly stirring in her bed. It was a special day for Shirin. Kamini and Kiara made slight movements here and there in a deliberate attempt to wake their mother up from her slumber. Shirin woke up with a smile and knew her darling girls were in the room. She was delighted to see Kamini and Kiara lovingly carry the breakfast tray decorated with a handmade Mother's Day card and a bunch of flowers in a small vase, along with the scrumptious breakfast meal prepared by her girls.

Kiara said with a grumpy face, "I wish Papa was here as well to enjoy this moment with us, Mamma."

Arjun had left for a business meeting and promised Shirin he would return soon to celebrate her birthday. Arjun had planned to throw a grand party and even decided the dress Shirin would wear for her birthday party—a long, red, flowing gown hand embroidered all over and loose enough not to accentuate her curves. This was certainly not Shirin's choice at all. She'd chosen a yellow, floral-printed knee-length dress with a flattering waist fit. Arjun was always particular about the dresses Shirin would wear for different occasions. He even kept track of her friend list and her social schedule. Shirin had to get everything approved by him, whether it was shopping for home requirements or her clothes. Shirin had always longed to make her own independent life decisions, but she couldn't take a stand firmly, with Arjun constantly interfering in all her choices.

While she was deeply immersed in her thoughts, Kamini and Kiara gently kept the tray on the breakfast table bedside, placed a little candle on a swirly cream muffin, and lit the candle for Shirin to blow.

"Make a wish, Mamma," said little Kiara, "And all your wishes will come true."

Shirin hugged her girls tightly and thought, '*When will the day come when I can make independent decisions without depending on Arjun for every piece of advice or opinion? My family members or Arjun will not judge me for taking the right step in all areas of my life.*' Arjun had always been possessive right from their college days. Still, Shirin was too innocent to realise that, and she thought it was very romantic and felt protected around Arjun. Gradually, it was stifling for her, especially when Arjun started to interfere too much in her daily affairs. Off late, he had been very busy and involved in his work. Due to his overly ambitious attitude, he was losing out on family time. Kiara and Kamini yearned to play with their father and longed for the family's fun times. What they enjoyed the most were the weekend outings and playing board games like Pictionary, Scrabble, and others.

Shirin noticed that for the past two months, Arjun had been preoccupied with something else in his mind that he wasn't ready to share with Shirin. She probed him a couple of times, but he snubbed her off.

Shirin's phone rang, and on the other end of the line was Roshani Didi. "Happy birthday, my darling sister! We've got to shop till we drop. This is your birthday shopping week. May God fulfil all your wishes and make all your dreams come true."

Shirin was happy to hear from her sister but sad at the same time since Arjun hadn't called her yet for a long time. Shirin was waiting for Arjun's call and wondered why he hadn't called. He was usually the first person to wish Shirin happy birthday. Shirin tried to call him on his phone, and his phone kept buzzing, but there was no response. She called their accountant, Mr Rajpal, and came to know that Arjun had to attend an urgent meeting in Mumbai. She was upset and angry about why he hadn't informed her about his long meetings.

Shirin heard a beep on her mobile, and Arjun was on the line. "Wishing you a belated happy birthday, my dear. I am sorry I couldn't call you earlier. I have just landed. I apologise for not informing you sooner, but I had to leave for an urgent meeting." Arjun sounded worried and was sweating profusely. "One tender got cancelled, and I had to be there to save the day, darling. I promise a big birthday bash, and your special gift awaits you. Have a wonderful day. I'll try to call back soon."

Shirin was still thinking about the briefcase that Arjun had mentioned. Shirin interrupted Arjun and asked hurriedly, "Did you find the black briefcase?"

"I have been looking for it everywhere. If you can find it, keep it safe," Arjun said before hanging up.

Suddenly, the doorbell rang, and a little bouquet of roses arrived. Shirin looked surprised and thought to herself, '*Who could have sent this?*'

The note read, "*I have dreamt of you since my yonder years. The thought of you warms my heart. Your smile is like the early morning delicate petals that adorn the beautiful grass with their colourful hues and fragrance. Your laughter is like a small child laughing her heart out, carefree and born free, oblivious to her surroundings and without a care in the world.*"

Shirin thought Arjun had sent this bouquet and the heart-touching note, but she looked closer and saw that the handwriting was different. Shirin wondered who it could be.

Meanwhile, Roshani Didi called again in a joyful mood and said, "Get ready in 10 minutes. I am coming with the driver. We will go shopping across the town, maybe to Koramangala."

Shirin ended the call but was haunted by the thought that it certainly wasn't Arjun who sent the bouquet. Then, who could it be? *'Well, I am sure I will get to know soon.'*

Chapter 4
Fate's Game

Arjun was always very punctual about his office timings, but today, he got a bit late to work. His mind was clouded with many worries and thoughts that had burnt him out over the week. He remembered that Shirin constantly enquired about the mysterious briefcase and knew he could not get away with it. Was it okay to let Shirin know what was bothering him, or should he not tell her? While contemplating, suddenly his phone rang, and he got worried and thought, *'Is it him calling? Mohanlal, the creditor.'* Arjun was relieved to know that it was Babulal, the driver, who called to ask if he could go back home and drive Shirin to the Bachpan Center, where she regularly visited to teach the slum children and taught tailoring to the women at the centre. Arjun knew that Shirin, on her birthday, would definitely take a day off and choose to go shopping. Arjun still wanted to call Shirin and know her plans. He wanted Babulal to take her wherever she wanted to go. Shirin always disliked the habit of Arjun, who often kept a strict vigil on her and her personal life.

It was a stormy night; the winds were howling while the trees swayed wildly with the wind's wrath. Sheets of rain began to gush down heavily, and the rain was drumming on the car's roof as Babulal was driving through the countryside to pick up Arjun from the airport. Babulal was struggling to drive through the storm and rain and knew he had to reach the airport on time to pick up Arjun as he was running late. Babulal managed to reach the airport and assumed he was late. He called Arjun to let him know that he had reached the airport, but his phone was switched off. Babulal thought that the flight might have been delayed and decided to wait patiently. Time was ticking, and it was quite late at night. It had stopped raining and was just drizzling.

Shirin called Babulal and sounded quite worried on the phone. "I have been trying to call Arjun sir so many times, but I wonder why his phone is switched off. I am getting really worried; can you please check at the airport information desk about flight no. 6E 5284 from Mumbai to Bangalore?"

Babulal went to the information desk to check on the flight and, on enquiring, he was told by the ground hostess that no one named Arjun had boarded flight 6E 5284. Babulal was astounded to hear this and again asked the ground staff to recheck the flight list. This time, the ground staff did a thorough check and called her senior manager on duty. The man came and cross-checked, and it turned out that Arjun had bought the ticket but never boarded the flight.

Babulal just could not believe that it was true. What could have possibly gone wrong? Shirin was frantically calling Babulal's phone to find out where Arjun was. He gathered his courage and called Shirin back to break the news. He didn't know what to tell her, and his head was reeling with pain.

"Madamji, I am calling from the airport's information desk, and I have been informed that Arjun sir never boarded the evening flight."

Shirin could not believe what she had heard. "What are you saying, Babulal?" Shirin sighed. "It can't be possible. He was supposed to get back tonight. You are mistaken; go and recheck with the ground staff. I am on my way to the airport now."

Shirin called for a cab and was on her way to the airport. It was still raining intermittently, and the light splash of rain kept bouncing off the window pane of the taxi. The city lights seemed to glimmer, and the city's bustling crowd captured Shirin's attention every time she drifted into a pensive mood. Shirin thought to herself that Arjun had promised her that he would come back home and organise a grand birthday party for her. As Shirin got closer to the airport, her heart fluttered with anxiety and fear about what was in store for her. As the taxi stopped in front of the airport, Shirin jumped out of the car and ran across to the information counter. She saw Babulal waiting there.

Shirin asked the lady at the information desk, "I have been told that my husband Arjun was supposed to board this flight, but he didn't board the flight. How is that even possible? He couldn't have vanished into thin air; this is bizarre." Shirin shook with nervousness and dread.

"Yes, ma'am. I regret to inform you that we don't know anything about him."

Shirin was in complete disbelief. She did not believe that this was happening to her. She took a deep breath and told Babulal, "Let's go home; the kids are waiting for me."

Shirin checked her messages, especially the last message sent by Arjun. "No matter what happens, you will tide through this; It's just a matter of time." Tears rolled down her cheeks.

What could have been the worst that could have happened to Arjun? Why didn't he let anyone know where he was? Shirin was worried and anxious as she struggled to accept the truth. Her entire world had changed. In which corner of the world would she look for Arjun, and what would she do?

Babulal drove Shirin home, and on the way, she asked Babulal to take her to the nearest police station so that they could report the matter of a missing person. They registered a complaint at the police station. The cop wasn't sure how long it would take to trace Arjun. Upon hearing this, Shirin just got up and walked to the car with heavy footsteps. It had finally stopped raining. It was a little chilly outside. She saw a cluster of people sipping tea on the roadside, merrily giggling and laughing together. She looked at them and thought to herself, '*I wish I could be carefree and happy just like them, but destiny has other plans for me.*'

Life is so uncertain and filled with trials and tribulations.

Life is like a boat sailing on the vast sea, and the waves of the sea are like the fate that rocks the boat.

We must yield to the winds of our fate as we sail through life's unexpected events.

Chapter 5
Breakdown

Little Kiara woke up in the morning rubbing her eyes and saw Shirin and Kamini hugging her tightly and whimpering softly. The room was dark, and Shirin hadn't drawn the curtains as she did ritually every morning. There was a little gap in the curtains, and the sun was bright outside, illuminating flora and fauna. In the distance, Kiara could see her best friend Tina walking towards the bus stop with a gaily paced step, joining her gang of friends. But the atmosphere in the room was sombre and dreary. The doorbell rang, and Babulal stood at the door with a briefcase. Shirin's head was dizzy from last night's trauma. She looked at the briefcase and remembered that this was the briefcase that Arjun was enquiring about.

"Mamma, what has happened to Papa? When will he come home?" asked Kiara.

Shirin stared sullenly out of the window without responding to her.

"We don't know what has happened to Papa and where he is."

As she hugged Kiara and Kamini, Shirin felt that her entire world had come tumbling down; her mind was blank and in chaos. She knew her happy and comfortable world was completely shattered. She wondered where he could possibly be.

Her phone rang, and it was Roshani on the line. "What has happened to you? You have not been responding to my calls."

Shirin said, "Arjun has been missing since last night. He never boarded the flight after his official board meeting got over in Mumbai."

Roshani couldn't believe her ears and said, "This is bizarre. We are on our way now to see you and the kids. I will inform Mom as well. You hang in there, sweetie."

The cops called Shirin and informed her that they called up the hotel reception at Leela to check when Arjun was last seen in the hotel room. Not much information could be retrieved from them.

Meanwhile, Roshani and her husband, Raman, reached Shirin's apartment. They both hugged the kids and Shirin tightly.

"Mummy is on her way from Lucknow, and she should be here by noon," said Roshani. "You have to be strong for your kids, my darling sister. They have their entire lives ahead of them. You have to be the pillar of strength for them."

Shirin was always dependent on Arjun, mentally and emotionally. She quit her job after Kamini was born and completely immersed herself in taking care of the kids although she wished she hadn't given up her lucrative career. Arjun's work made him travel extensively. She was a dedicated mother who gave a lot of time to her children. When she would see people going to work during the day, her heart longed to get back to her job, but the fear of leaving her children with the maid changed her mind. She admired mothers who could juggle home and family so well. Somehow, she felt she wasn't ready to take on that kind of responsibility yet. She knew Arjun always wanted her to care for the kids and give them all her time. Arjun took all the major decisions in the house, and she never felt confident enough to make the decisions alone. She would always lean on Arjun for his suggestions, and now, she was at a crossroads, wondering how to move on from here.

All her bitter and sweet memories were coming back. There was a flood of emotions, and it seemed like a movie flashing by. She remembered the day when Arjun celebrated the first business assignment by taking Shirin out. Since they were saving every little penny, he decided to enjoy street food with Shirin by eating *pani puri* from the roadside chaat *wala* in the main market. The aroma of a crunchy, oil-drenched potato patty that was freshly fried tickled their nostrils. As they wanted to save every bit of money, pani puri was the cheapest treat they could have happily enjoyed together. The vendor dished out a bowl to the couple, and before they could take a bite, crunch it up, and savour the sweet and sour flavour of pani puri, the vendor dished out the second one in no time with dexterity.

The tangy, spicy concoction of water from the crunchy water balls was trickling down from the corner of their mouths, and Shirin remembered how both of them laughed till the cool water trickled down her cleavage that wet her kurta. He stepped closer to Shirin and wiped her mouth with his hanky. She felt comforted and came close to him as she bent over to adjust her dupatta. Her silky hair brushed across his face, and the warmth of her touch stirred his emotions.

He hugged her tight, and she said with embarrassment, "What are you doing? People are watching."

Arjun said, "No one has the time to look around, and no one dares look at my beautiful wife."

Shirin blushed on hearing this, and he held her hand tight. It was a moment of joy for both Arjun and Shirin when their first assignment came through. Arjun started small as a textile trading and manufacturing company. He tried to spend as much time as possible with Shirin when he began his new venture, but as the days passed and the business started growing, he got busy and neck-deep in his work with very little time for family. He slowly turned into a workaholic. When Kamini was born, Arjun had more time to play with her, but he could not give Kiara much attention as the business expanded. Shirin also felt lonely at times when Arjun had to travel for long business trips. She found it difficult to take care of the kids all by herself with no family support or even domestic help. It was the beginning of her struggle. She relied on Arjun emotionally when it came to making decisions about the kids or the house. She was completely shattered and wondered how she would manage now that she was alone.

The doorbell rang. Kamini answered the door and it was Roshani at the door. Roshani hugged Kamini and walked inside the house. Roshani came towards Shirin, hugged her and said, "I have been thinking about you and the kids all throughout since the time I heard about Arjun. It's time for you to take charge of your home and your kids. Are you ready? You don't have a choice at this juncture."

Shirin still couldn't believe that all this had happened so quickly. She was feeling very weak in her heart, and her head felt very heavy under the weight of all this emotional turmoil. The journey ahead for her would be arduous and full of trials and tribulations. She had no clue about the investments made by Arjun in the stock market; Arjun always handled all the bank details.

Shirin's mother had arrived in the meantime and hugged the children tightly as soon as they entered the house. Her mother hugged Shirin and the kids and said, "I am there to support you, my child. Why don't you all move to Lucknow? At my age, I can't relocate; you know it's difficult."

Shirin just cried and didn't know what to say. She knew moving to Lucknow and leaving the house, the kid's school, and the business wasn't feasible. The activities outside the house went by like any other day: sweeping of the street by the sweeper, honking of the cars, and children playing noisily outside the park. Everything appeared to be normal, except for the moody atmosphere inside the house that was sullen, which was contrasted by the sparrows singing and darting across the potted plants, people walking along the road, and in the distance, a group of college students laughing aloud. There was a feeling of emptiness and solitude inside the house. Shirin was angry towards Arjun for what he had done to them. Bitterness and resentment toward him were brewing inside her. How could he leave his family? Why did he do this? Shirin was reeling under her thoughts.

You have robbed us of those priceless times spent together.

You have utterly duped me.

You have broken my heart, and I feel completely betrayed by you.

Chapter 6
The Briefcase

The girls terribly missed their dad. Kamini was sobbing in a corner, her beady eyes swimming in tears. Kiara was sobbing with her head pressed in her mamma's arms and was shaking with suppressed sobs. Kiara strolled around in her room since she hadn't been to school and took her favourite doll to Shirin's room.

"Papa bought this doll for me last year and bought Didi her basketball kit. I miss Papa so much."

As Shirin hugged her, she saw the black briefcase that the driver, Babulal, had given to her in the corner. All this time, Shirin was completely heartbroken and not in control of herself. The air was heavy enough to create drag in her steps, and she wondered what could be in the briefcase. After looking closely, Shirin realised that it was the same suitcase that Babulal had handed over after returning from their memorable trip in the foothills of the Himalayas. Their last family vacation was in the North East's lush green valleys and breath-taking scenic views.

Shirin tried to open the briefcase, but it seemed to have a lock code. She wondered what could be in the briefcase that Arjun did not tell her about. She tried several combinations, including his year of birth, their anniversary date, and her date of birth, but she could not break the code. Shirin was contemplating in her mind what could possibly be in the briefcase. Shirin thought to herself, '*Why don't I try putting Kamini's date of birth?*' The combination was right, and the briefcase opened with the perfect click. She rummaged through the papers and saw many neatly-filed documents in different folders. Her eyes were still heavy, and she had a throbbing pain in her head from all the emotional turmoil. She had to strain her eyes to read the documents in detail. There was a file with a few official documents, original copies of several shares, and the company's power of attorney. She then chanced upon an envelope with her name written: Shirin, a message for you. It looked like Arjun's handwriting. Her mind was reeling with all the thoughts about these official documents and why they were all put in a briefcase like this. She opened the envelope addressed to her.

"Dear Shirin,

The first time I saw you, my heart knew you were my soulmate and we were destined for each other. The innocence in your eyes and the warmth of your smile melted my heart like the winter snow that melts with the sun's brightness. Like the bright sun, your cheerful smile would always bring happiness to my heart. Despite so much opposition from my parents, you decided to marry me, and that became my strength. You gave me two beautiful girls, who are our blessing from the Almighty. Kamini and Kiara are very loving, and may Almighty always protect them.

When I started my garment manufacturing business from scratch, I could not invest much money, and we struggled financially. As the business grew, I approached more investors to expand my business into an empire. I invested a significant part of my earnings in the stock market, not realising that I was taking a huge risk. With a heavy heart, I want to tell you that I have lost all my money in the stock market. All the money that I invested in our business is lost. The K & K company we named after our daughters is in huge debt. The creditors and the workers have been hounding me. I filed for bankruptcy because I was afraid to face my family and the rest of society. I believe in your inner strength, and I know you will sail ahead in the tumultuous journey of life. I am not in the right state of mind and ashamed to face all of you. You have the qualifications and the capability to steer ahead. There is a complete mess and chaos out there that I cannot deal with at all. I am forever going away from all of you. This briefcase has all the original official documents of the company. I feel like a coward running away from life's challenges, but I just don't have the strength to deal with all this anymore.

I love you, Kiara, and Kamini with all my heart.

Love Arjun."

When life throws huge challenges at us, how do we encounter them?

Should we flee or make a bold move forward?

Move on, my friend, with a strong resolve, and do not give in to failure.

Even on a stormy day, trees stand tall and deeply rooted, no matter how much the wind tries to destroy them.

Despite all the obstacles, we must remain firm and unyielding and courageously advance.

Chapter 7
Building Moments of Strength

Shirin gathered her thoughts and decided it was time to take control of the situation rather than wallow in regret. There was no turning back for her. She had to move on. She got Kiara and Kamini dressed for school and told them to be strong.

She hugged Kamini and Kiara and said, "My dear girls, you must be strong in your heart; we shall sail through together."

Shirin called her mom and asked if she could stay with them for a few days since she needed her mom's support. After the kids left for school, Shirin called for Babulal, and he drove her to the office of K & K Company. Shirin walked into the office immediately to meet the senior VP, Mr Harsh Tripathi, who was in a meeting with the staff. On seeing Shirin, he excused himself from the meeting and quickly dashed out of the board room.

"I am very sorry to hear about Mr Arjun. I wonder what could have happened to him."

Harsh was a tall man with a sharp intellect and penetrating eyes. His salt-and-pepper hair showed years of experience, confidence, and maturity.

With a smile, Harsh looked at Shirin and said, "Are you aware that the company is in the doldrums and many staff members have already left? I cannot hold the fort for too long as well. I have already put in my papers."

Shirin looked at him, trying to keep a straight face, and said, "I know this will not be easy for me, but I am determined to face this challenge."

Shirin organised a meeting with the company's CA to learn about the company's losses. Creditors and investors were constantly calling and demanding payments. She called the lawyer to initiate bankruptcy proceedings. She knew this wouldn't be easy for her and that she had to grit her teeth and brace herself for the hard times to come. As Shirin was about to leave the office, she saw a painting of a huge ship sailing in the sea, trying to survive the storm with waves lashing, yet, the ship stood erect without sinking, giving hope that no matter what challenges we may face, we have to stand boldly amid a storm and not surrender to the situation. Shirin realised that now, she had to gather all her strength and open a new chapter in her life. She thought of starting her own business, which she would build with hard work, and give the company a new name, "Spindle Wheels Private Limited."

Shirin always wanted to work for the benefit of the workers as the weavers were exploited by the middlemen. While working for a clothing company before marriage, Shirin discovered that weavers were poorly paid. The nine-yard saree draped by models and celebrities is showcased worldwide and adorned by the rich and famous, but every piece woven by the weaver has a sad story to tell. Abject poverty had forced many weavers to abandon their craft and look for other jobs in the city. Shirin always loved colours and fabric, but somewhere, she decided she wanted to give more time to her children and enjoy the comfort of her home and her pleasure time. She had made this choice, and over the years, she had surrendered to Arjun's domineering nature. She thought life was telling her to be courageous and take on this challenge head-on. '*I have to be strong and set an example for my girls.*' If life throws a challenge at you, will you give up or gather your strength to move on?

There were many worries looming over her head. How will the funding be handled for the new company? How will she travel to the distant villages, leaving her two daughters at home? Will her mom agree to move in with them? Many questions reeled in her head, and she could feel her stomach fluttering. She took a deep breath and remembered what her father always told her: "Hardships are part and parcel of life. Be brave and believe in your immense potential. You are capable of achieving anything and everything if you do not give up on your journey of life midway."

Chapter 8
A Stranger's Note

At home, Kiara and Kamini had come back from school, walking back from the bus stand with heavy footsteps.

"The house is so empty without Papa," said Kiara.

Kamini snapped out of it and said, "You've got to deal with it, young girl. We have no choice. So, get used to it from now on." Kamini felt bad after having said that.

Meanwhile, the doorbell rang, and the security guard held a letter for Shirin. Her mom, Sheela, received the letter and wondered who could have sent a letter to Shirin. It was 5 p.m.; Shirin had just returned after a long day at the office trying to settle matters with the CA and the company lawyer.

"How was your day?" asked Shirin's mom.

"Ma, I am very exhausted and don't know where to begin; my head is throbbing with pain, and I would love a cup of chai."

Sheela got up to go to the kitchen and asked Shanti, the cook, to make tea for everyone. Sheela thought to herself, *'Poor child! What a carefree life she lived, and suddenly she is amidst all this turmoil. I wonder if she can handle all this pressure and keep up with the unseen challenges. God, give her strength!* The aroma of the Darjeeling tea filled the living room, and Shirin was reminded of the beautiful memories of the trip to the North East with Arjun and the kids. Life is so uncertain, and so are people. She could not even think it was the last trip with Arjun, and she was unaware of his intentions.

Sheela looked at the envelope, and the name looked unfamiliar. Sheela knitted her brows and shrugged, wondering who could have given the letter and the packet to the security guard. According to the guard, a *saheb* arrived in a small white car and handed him the letter and package, instructing him to deliver them to Shirin madam. She handed over the letter and the packet to her daughter. Shirin was in a different state of mind, deeply immersed in her thoughts about the new venture that she had been thinking about. She looked at the envelope, and the handwriting looked familiar. She tried to recall and suddenly remembered that she had received a bouquet on her birthday, thinking Arjun had sent it to her, but it was someone else, and yes, the handwriting matched this stranger. *'I wonder who this man is who has sent me flowers on my birthday and now a letter with a packet.'* Shirin opened the package and saw a beautiful hand-embroidered stole. Shirin's mother noticed the stole and warned her not to accept strangers' gifts.

"I know, Ma, but I don't know who this guy is," Shirin replied, "I'm not in the mood to accept any gifts."

But she was curious to know what was in the letter.

"Dear Shirin,

You are going through the toughest phase of your life, but remember to believe in your power and be fearless. Trials and tribulations may await you, but if you overcome your fear and hold your head high then problems will only appear as challenges. Remember the power that moves the sun, the earth, and the trees—the same power lies within you. The road ahead might be filled with difficulties, but remember not to give in to your weakness because therein lies your victory. I will always be watching over you, and I completely believe in your inner power and confidence. I am your secret admirer, and remember, I will and have always loved you with all my heart."

Shirin thought to herself, '*I wonder who this man is who showed up at a time when I am in deep trouble.*'

Shirin picked up the receiver and called the society's guard, "Ramu Bhaiya, next time anyone hands you over a letter or a package, please don't receive it; tell the person to deliver it to me personally."

Somewhere in her heart, Shirin felt comforted and encouraged after reading the letter sent by the stranger. She was still trying to get over the anger and resentment brewing inside her against Arjun.

Chapter 9
Crossroads

Shirin knew that she had to build her life all over again. It would not be an easy task, but she was determined. There was a new surge of hope. Sometimes, she doubted her capabilities, thinking, 'I have never handled a business; where do I start?' In school, Kamini and Kiara's teachers were taking extra care that Kamini and Kiara should be able to focus on their studies. Their teachers constantly involved them in one class activity or another.

Kamini did not have a lot of friends in school as she was very choosy about whom she could befriend.

Aditi, a chirpy, bubbly girl who was her classmate in school, told her one day when Kamini and Aditi were sitting together during lunchtime, "Why don't you plan a trip during summer break with me? I will be visiting my grandparents, who live in Goa. I love the beach and always look forward to visiting my grandparents in Goa. It's going to be a lot of fun. Come along!"

Kamini was still recovering emotionally and missed her dad a lot.

"Well, I am not sure; I will have to ask my mom. Give me some time to think, Aditi."

"Great! Take your time, but remember I am always there for you as your best friend."

Her words were comforting for Kamini. She walked out of the classroom and headed straight for the basketball court. She dribbled her basketball alone in the middle of the court and recalled the joyful moments of playing basketball with her dad on a family holiday together. Aditi came to the basketball court looking for Kamini, worried about why she had suddenly disappeared. She could see pearls of sweat dripping down the side of Kamini's face. Aditi watched as Kamini ran up to the basketball and threw the ball. It hit the rim and fell off the basket. Aditi stepped aside in time and saw Kamini catch and reshoot the ball. This time, it hit the backboard.

On her third attempt for a shot in the basket, Kamini hit the ball hard as if trying to tell herself that life is unfair, but I have to move on; the ball bounced on the backboard again, and then it landed on the ring and popped out of the basket.

Kamini jumped with joy and screamed, "Yes! I did it this time." Kamini took a deep breath.

Aditi could hear it from the other side of the court. Kamini placed her bag on her back and walked over to Aditi. Kamini and Aditi smiled at each other and walked to their classroom.

***

Sitting on her garden chair at 7 a.m., Shirin could hear the wind rustling and see the sparrows and doves flitting across her potted plants. The chirp and the birds' twitter were no longer music to her ears since she was getting restless and worried about her new venture. She had mixed emotions, thinking that this was a new chapter in her life where she would embark on a new journey by starting her own business.

She was immersed in her thoughts, thinking about Arjun and his sudden betrayal. Why did he do this? Where could he be? Should I call his dear friend, Madhav, to find out just in case he has any clue about Arjun? Shirin picked up her phone and wrote a message. "Did Arjun call you in the last couple of days? He has not been responding to any messages and we have filed a police complaint as well." She sent a WhatsApp message to Madhav and was anxiously waiting for him to respond.

Madhav called and said in a tense voice, "What happened, Shirin? Where is Arjun? I hope you and the kids are fine. I have been travelling out of the country for a month and haven't been in touch with Arjun for a long time. If you need any help at all, please let me know. I will be back by next week and will certainly connect with you again. I tried calling Arjun but his number is not reachable."

Shirin was going through a difficult time handling the creditors. It was a daunting task for her, and she constantly brainstormed the different strategies she would need to employ single-handedly. To top it all off, her creditors were constantly hounding her to pay off the mounting debts that Arjun had created by borrowing a lot from the bank and being unable to pay the interest. Arjun could not handle the mounting debts, and his company, K & K Comp., filed for bankruptcy. Shirin was enraged by Arjun's cowardice and the fact that he had to abandon them and simply vanish from the face of the earth. She knew it was time for her to rise up and not give in to difficult times. While she could have lived a carefree life completely reliant on Arjun for everything, she would now have to make her own decisions.

During her years before marriage, working in the apparel company, she had worked with weavers in Andhra Pradesh. When she heard about their unimaginable plight and poverty, somewhere in her heart, she wished to help them somehow. Shirin got an idea while sipping her aromatic, freshly brewed tea. While she was in a pensive mood, she decided that she would trade with the weavers from the south and would certainly make efforts to give them a better life.

Chapter 10
New Beginnings

Little Kiara missed her dad a lot and often questioned her grandma about his homecoming.

"Nani, when will papa come home? I miss him so much."

Shirin's mom knew she would have to spend more time with her grandchildren and couldn't think of returning to her hometown for some time. Sheela hugged little Kiara tightly and took her to the balcony outside, near the bird feeder.

"Come, let's feed the birds and squirrels. Also, bring your dolls to play on the balcony, and then we will sit down to complete your homework."

"Nani, I am in no mood to play or study at all; I miss Papa a lot."

Kamini had come back from school by then. "Why did you miss school today, Kiara?"

Kiara sat on her little chair in the playroom and, with a grumpy look on her face, exclaimed, "I miss Papa a lot, and Mama also isn't home."

Kamini walked up to Kiara and piped up her voice in a serious tone, "You know that Papa is missing, and we don't know where he is. God keep him safe wherever he may be. I miss him a lot, but as Mama said, we can't brood over it and must move on with our daily affairs."

Nani looked at the two girls and hugged them. She wanted to divert their attention and thought of pepping them up. "Okay, my darlings, I've prepared special snacks that are tasty and crunchy, just like you girls like it; wash your hands and hurry over to the table."

Kamini and Kiara were hungry as it was time for their evening snack, and they could not resist the mouth-watering, salty crackers that Sheela had made for them. As Sheela opened the jar full of crackers, their aroma filled the room, and the brown, crispy crackers seemed irresistible. As Kiara took a crunchy bite, she savoured every bit of the delectable cracker. Kamini couldn't stop praising Nani for the most delicious crackers made lovingly by Sheela for her granddaughters.

"Nani, you must make more snacks like this; I simply love them." Kamini tried to finish her sentence with a mouthful of it.

The doorbell suddenly rang, and Shirin entered the house looking tired and drained after a long day. She had gotten back to work after a long break. For the first time in so many days, the house seemed chirpy with the commotion of Kamini and Kiara arguing and giggling together.

"Look, Mamma is home!" exclaimed Kiara.

Shirin smiled at the girls and said, "I can't wait to have what you all have been nibbling. It looks yummy!"

"Nani made the most delicious crackers. You will love them, Mummy."

Shirin sat at the dining table, enjoying her evening snack and freshly brewed filter coffee. She felt happy for the first time in so many days that things seemed to be returning to normal, hopefully, since Arjun had left them. Shirin wanted to share her plans with the kids and her mom but didn't know where to start.

"Mamma, I need to travel to the interiors of Andhra Pradesh regarding the new business I am planning to set up. It is not an easy decision to travel out of town, leaving the girls behind, but I have to do this to start my new venture successfully."

Shirin's mom didn't look very happy, as she knew it would be a lot of responsibility for her to take care of the two girls.

"Don't worry, Mom. I will take little Kiara with me because she cannot stay without me for long."

Shirin's mom looked worried and said, "Beta, it's not easy staying in a village with a little girl; how safe would that be? Just give up that idea."

Shirin looked at her mother lovingly and said, "I will think about what you said, Mamma." Shirin got up from her chair, smiled, and affectionately kept her hands on her mother's soft shoulder. Shirin held her hand and warmly kissed them, "Look, Mamma, don't worry at all. When I spoke to Roshani Didi about this, she told me I could stay in their company guest house. What's worrying you? Come on; this is not the same Shirin who always had to depend on Arjun for every decision to be made. Now,

I must think independently and make quick decisions for the family's well-being."

Shirin's mom looked at her with a warm, loving smile and said, "My dear girl, why can't you send someone else for this work? Why do you have to go? What about the kid's school?"

Shirin hugged her mom lovingly, rested her chin on her shoulder, and said, "Don't worry, Ma. I have spoken to Kiara and Kamini's teachers; they will keep me updated about all the class and homework assignments from time to time whenever I will be travelling. Her school teachers are very cooperative and helpful. Listen, mama, I have to look at cost-cutting as well; I can't be employing someone else for this work and paying a salary to him, and also, this is my baby, and I want to start my new business single-handedly and nurture it slowly."

Shirin inhaled deeply, grinned at her kids, and realised that it would not be an easy road for her, but she was determined to give it a start and take the plunge wholeheartedly. It would take her some time to overcome the fact that Arjun suddenly left her and the kids to face these difficult times. It was a deep wound that would take a long time to heal.

Time is the best healer, and as the moments go by,

It reminds us that everything changes with the passage of time.

And nothing stays the same forever.

Time is a great healer.

That soothes painful memories

and heals open wounds and broken hearts.

Time is the best teacher who guides us through life's ups and downs.

So, trust time and believe in your limitless potential to overcome life's highs and lows.

Chapter 11
The Journey Begins

Shirin's mother baked flaky aloo parathas and chickpeas for breakfast and served them with yoghurt. The sitting room was filled with the aroma of crispy paratha. Shirin rushed into the kitchen because she needed to catch a train. The side of the kitchen stove was illuminated by the radiant sun that streamed through the kitchen window. Shirin's mother tenderly heaped a lovely breakfast onto her dish.

"I'll have to skip lunch if I devour everything in sight," Shirin said.

She was aware that for the ensuing several days, she would not be able to eat anything from her home. Shirin changed her mind at the last minute. She decided to leave Kiara in the care of her mother. It was the best thing to do for Kiara.

"I miss Papa so much. I wish he was there," Kiara whimpered and frowned.

Kamini looked at Shirin and said, "Why did Papa leave us and go? Did we say anything to upset him?"

The look in Kamini's eyes melted Shirin's heart. She lovingly looked at her girls and stepped closer to them to give them a tight hug. As Shirin put her arms around them, she said in a strong voice, "I can't answer that question but I guess he has gone to a place that we don't know of. We have to be strong for each other." Having said that, Shirin and the girls embraced each other in a group hug.

"Mamma, we love you very much," said Kamini and Kiara together.

"Be very good, girls; both of you, and don't bother Nani. I will be back soon," Shirin stated as she waved at them standing at the entrance door.

Shirin was informed by Babulal, who had just arrived at the porch, that they would need to head to the station quickly. She prepared her suitcase and said goodbye to everyone. "Don't worry about me; I'll phone you when I get here."

The suitcase was taken by Babulal and placed in the vehicle's trunk. Shirin left the house and immediately noticed the cold and crisp morning. She embraced herself and adjusted her shrug to feel more comfortable and warmer while the morning dew's sweet, yielding aroma cascaded around her. The mailbox outside the house caught her eye just as she was getting ready to enter the car. She approached the envelope blowing in the breeze to look at the message, *"As you go on a new voyage."* Shirin was astonished and questioned how the letter had ended up there. She also saw that the handwriting appeared to be familiar.

"We are running late, Madamji; let's leave," Babulal said when he intervened.

Shirin hurriedly climbed into the car and began her new journey. Her feelings were stirred by the prospect of leaving her children with her mother for a few days. She pondered how she would balance her domestic duties with starting a new business. She frequently thought she was nothing more than a sponge, sopped full of human emotions because everything was occurring swiftly. She thought back to the times when she didn't have to worry about money or Arjun's business. After taking a few sips of water and resting her head on the backrest of the car's back seat, she felt her throat dry. She wondered why Arjun had to be a coward and abandon them when she was thinking about him. They were drawing from their savings, and she needed to set aside cash to launch her business.

She was contemplative and suddenly focused on the white envelope she had taken from the mailbox. She wanted to know what was in the letter. She pursed her lips and smiled slightly as she gently tore the envelope's edges. Was she interested in learning to whom this stranger was addressing her letters? She was healing from the emotional scars caused by Arjun abruptly abandoning her and the daughters and disappearing into thin air. She brushed that idea aside. She decided that she did not wish to think about men.

In the letter, it said,

"Dear Shirin,

Like the vast, open ocean, life has obstacles and surprises. As we stroll along the beach, happily gathering shells of all shapes and sizes, we have no idea what will come into our collection. We have to decide what the ocean has to give and move on. There will be many ups and downs along the path, but we can't give up. I have faith in your tremendous power and potential. You simply cannot be stopped. Have faith in yourself and step out on faith, as you did when you read my letter without dissecting it. You won't lose hope if you follow your instinct and conviction, which are powerful and pure. Instead, you'll reach your target and clear the way for your daughters. I have faith in your prodigious abilities. You are the picture of beauty and strength, and you will succeed in all your future attempts.

Your devoted admirer!"

'*Who is this man, and why won't he divulge his identity?*' Shirin pondered. Why did he always show up when she needed direction and support and seemed so worried about her? She was able to sense her face's warmth and heartbeat. The sun's rays enhanced the radiance on her face as they entered the automobile through a window. She experienced a sense of value and desire for the first time in many years. It was something that, with Arjun nearby, she hadn't experienced in a while. The care was completed.

Babulal called to Shirin when she was lost in contemplation, "Madamji, we have reached. Please move quickly and carefully. We are running late; we must hurry before the train arrives at the platform; let's get there," in the tone of a stern, elderly father.

"I'm sorry, but I won't be able to give you your pay until the end of the month, but I'll definitely transfer the money to your account," Shirin remarked while giving Babulal a tender glance.

"I'm not only working for money, Madamji. I care for you and your family," Babulal replied as he pulled the suitcase from the boot of the automobile and gave a pleasant smile to Shirin. "I've started doing regular work; I owe you a lot, and I won't stop doing anything I can to help you just because you can't pay me. Madamji, if you ever need to travel a long way, give me a call."

"I feel blessed to have you around," Shirin stated with a loving grin as she spoke to Babulal.

They then began to make their way towards platform number 3 of the railway station. Shirin quickened her pace in order to board the train on time. Shirin got on to the train that would take her to Warangal. The train slowly chugged out of the station and Shirin was ready to embark on her new journey.

Chapter 12
The Weavers' Hub

The morning sky had a rosy tint from the summer sun, and sunlight poured in through Shirin's guest room window on her warm cheeks. Shirin woke up early in the morning to the sun's brilliant rays. Shirin was very lazy to get up but she knew that she was on a short business trip and wanted to utilize her two days very well.

She grabbed her mobile device to call home.

"Hello!"

Shirin's mother answered the landline.

"Yes, who's that?"

"Ma, it's me, Shirin," interjected Shirin. "How are the girls doing? I hope they are not troubling you, mama?"

Shirin's mum smiled and said that the girls are no trouble at all. In fact, Kamini and Kiara had just left for school. Shirin's mother waved at the girls as they passed the home's front door. "Everything is OK here, my sweetheart; just focus on your work. I am taking good care of everything here." Shirin's mother reassured her that she didn't need to worry.

Suddenly, there was a knock on the door that interrupted their conversation. Shirin hung up the phone.

"Yes, who is it?"

A plump man with a smile on his face – the caretaker – stood at the door holding the breakfast table. "Memsaab, your cup of tea and breakfast is here."

Shirin asked him to keep the tray. She got out of bed and straightened her nightgown with a bit of discomfort.

Shirin said in an irritated voice, " Aren't you suppose to knock before coming inside? Now, come in."

The man looked around the room and saw the scattered suitcases with clothes. She wanted him to leave.

"You can go now. Thank you!" Shirin leaned her head back and thought to herself that life was so comfortable with no worries until that dreadful evening when Arjun suddenly left them. Shirin knew she couldn't waste much time thinking because she had to hastily return home in two days while on a brief business trip to the city of Warangal.

As soon as Shirin finished her quick shower and breakfast, she changed into a clean lemon-yellow salwar kameez. She looked beautiful and dazzling in her attire. She admired herself by looking in the mirror. She wasn't in that mood for long and she had spent the entire time worrying. She was unprepared for the future.

The plan for her company's layout was complete, but she was flooded with many thoughts about her business and daughters. Shirin knew the market trends and the challenges they posed, and she knew that it would not be easy to set up a business all by herself. Also, she knew she had to move on and work very hard on expanding her business.

She was aware of the reason for her visit to Warangal and intended to buy some old and antique clothes that were so popular in the larger towns. She was ready to take a stroll around the town's loom byways to know more about the place. Shirin looked at her handbag and a tiny black diary which had all the important numbers of weavers and dealers. She waited at the bus stand in the scorching summer heat for a while and spotted an old, dusty bus overflowing with passengers. She was hesitant to board the bus after seeing how crowded it was. Shirin changed her mind and opted to wait for an auto because the bus appeared very crowded.

As she left the guest house, she waited in the sweltering heat with billowing dust clouds and suddenly spotted an auto in the distance. She boarded the rickety old autorickshaw.

The driver asked Shirin, "Madamji, where are you from, and what brings you to our city?"

She wasn't in the mood to converse with the stranger, so she furrowed her brows. She turned her attention away from the driver and looked at the opposite side. The jarring ride and billowing dust cloud made Shirin cough and scowl. Shirin knew it would be difficult to start a new business independently, but she had gritted her teeth and knew there was no turning back. Shirin had just started her firm and was unsure of her ability to compete with the weavers and other major market players.

The sun dropped, and the sky blazed, blushed, and dimmed for nearly an hour. Shirin was drenched in sweat and extremely thirsty. '*I ought to have dressed more casually rather than wearing a clean kurta. It's all dirty now.*' Shirin was pushed aside by an odd-looking young man brushing up against her at the bus stand.

"One minute. You can't sit properly for once?" Shirin remarked with a harsh expression.

The man gave Shirin a stern look, grinned wryly, and leaned close to her. Shirin's attractive looks always caught everybody's attention. Shirin exited the vehicle and started looking for another route to the weaver's alley because she didn't want to quarrel with the stranger.

Every painful step was accompanied by the searing sensation of the scorching ground against Shirin's delicate feet. The sweltering summer heat had completely drained her out physically but her strong iron will seemed undaunted and she quickened her pace.

That was unlike anything Shirin had ever encountered. Shirin longed to get back home. This wouldn't be an easy task for her. Stray cattle constantly blocked the alley and byways, making the entire area look like a maze. Shirin couldn't figure out which gully to take. She searched her handbag for her official mini diary.

Shirin opened her diary and looked for the weaver Zulfikar's home phone number and address, whom she needed to meet as he was the best in his profession. Shirin's college friend who worked in the fashion industry had given Zulfikar's contact number. She tightened her handbag and thought, '*I have never experienced anything like this in my life. This is not going to be an easy journey at all.*'

Shirin walked outside and stretched after the arduous trip. She had doubts at the moment and was frequently worried about whether this endeavour would be successful. Shirin got into a narrow lane as she was looking for Zulfikar's house.

After emerging from his dilapidated mud-brick house, an old man with glasses asked Shirin a few questions.

"I have come from the city of Bangalore to meet Zulfikarji, the skilled weaver," Shirin smiled and told the old man, trying to manage her feelings of optimism and dread.

The old man had a perplexed expression.

"Is this house number 42? "Shirin asked him while grinning at him. "The most accomplished and gifted weaver, Zulfikar, I suppose, resides at this place." Shirin enquired. "May I address you as Zulfikar Ji?" Shirin asked with a smile.

"Please don't use the word accomplished since I still have a long way to go and haven't reached that level," said Zulfikar with a smile.

The elderly man, Zulfi, led her inside; although the interior was clean, the walls appeared pale, and the ceiling had cracks. The room smelled musty as the radio played old Hindi classic songs by Mohammad Rafi. The kitchen ceiling was stained with soot, and the corners of the walls were cobweb-covered. Zulfikar looked at Shirin and called her to the room where his ailing wife was continuously coughing.

"My wife has been suffering from tuberculosis, and I don't have enough money for her treatment."

Shirin looked at the old man and said, "I want to build my new company on a foundation of trust and understanding between us, and I want to make sure that you make a good profit and have enough money to treat your wife as best you can."

Shirin smiled as she looked at the old loom, on which a brilliant fuchsia-pink silk cloth was half-woven.

As the weaver combines the warp and weft to create a gorgeous, attention-grabbing fabric that captures our attention, we must trust the challenges that life throws at us and recognise that we are the designers of the fabric of our own lives.

Chapter 13
A Close Encounter

In addition to wanting to support the underprivileged weavers in whatever way she could, Shirin wanted to highlight the rich tradition of the Indian weavers. After meeting Zulfikar and observing the community's hardship, Shirin made the decision to work directly with the weavers rather than through middlemen so that the benefit would go to the weavers. She had been speaking with several weavers in the community to learn about their financial struggles. Shirin needed to travel frequently for her business to buy handloom textiles for fashion products. She had developed an excellent rapport with the weavers. She considered meeting Kamla, who was well-known in the village for her gorgeous needlework and delicate work on silk Mori, but she had a night-time train to catch. Shirin knew that she had to utilise her time well. Shirin had an early appointment with Kamla and decided to meet her in the early hours of the morning.

A dilapidated mud brick house with an old Banyan tree with rich foliage greeted Shirin. Shirin was always on time and was a stickler for time. Shirin appeared attractive in a cotton kurta, her hair was neatly tied back, and she wore an optimistic look on her face. Shirin was greeted by Kamla, a bespectacled woman in her seventies with wrinkled skin and brown lips.

"Madam, what brings you here?" Kamla said while grinning slightly.

She welcomed Shirin inside her tiny house. Kamla offered her a place to sit. Shirin sat carefully on a low settee. Shirin looked around and her nose was tickled by the aroma of cooking emanating from the kitchen's soot-filled chimney.

Shirin looked at Kamla with a smile and said, "I want to support the weaving communities and give them the tools they need to pursue their vocations." Shirin smiled at Kamla.

"We have taken loans from money lenders and are groaning under poverty to repay them with interest," Kamla stated as she sent a doubtful glance Shirin's way. "Because of our ignorance and lack of understanding, intermediaries and moneylenders frequently take advantage of us." The lines on Kamla's cheeks and the cracks in her hands demonstrated how laboriously and carefully each piece of fabric is embellished with elaborate embroidery work. "Madamji, although the demand for our labour is high and customers are willing to pay high prices, it is the wealthy businessman who makes profits, and we receive no payment for our efforts."

Shirin reassured Kamla as she smiled and turned to face her that she would do everything in her power to assist the weaving community.

But she was unable to persuade Kamla. "Madamji, it's hard to trust people from the city. We are straightforward villagers who only desire to toil hard and get the rewards for our effort; we reject empty promises."

Shirin parted her lips and knitted her brows. She then took a step back and retraced her steps. She was aware that she would need to be patient in order to gain the villagers' trust. Shirin might find it difficult to regain their faith after the middleman's years of exploitation of them, but she was not going to give in quickly. She would have to put in much effort to develop her textile company.

Shirin was prepared to catch the early morning train back to Bangalore and was happy with the thought that she would be reunited with her daughters at home the next day. She always eagerly anticipated her visits to Warangal. Shirin was put off by the bumpy ride in the auto-rickshaw as she was being driven to the train station on a warm July afternoon. After she boarded the train and was comfortably seated in the coupe, Shirin looked outside the window of her train and saw the vada seller chit-chatting with the ice cream seller and having a good laugh together. Under the old mango tree next to the wooden bench on the platform, a pile of dried, lifeless leaves was picked up by a whirlwind. As they twisted, turned, and danced in the wind, the leaves gave the impression of dancing in the wind. Slowly, the train pulled out of the station at a snail's pace. As the train chugged out of the station, Shirin smiled at the thought of going back home to her daughters and her mother. Clouds in the shape of candy floss looked like they were floating over the bright blue heavens. The view of lush paddy fields with tiny mud-brick houses that dotted the green fields and farmers busily cultivating crops in the scorching heat caught Shirin's attention.

Shirin always looked forward to taking the flight sometimes so that she could quickly reach home. She wished she could fly to different locations, but she was limited by her ability to afford an expensive flight ticket. In her heart, she knew that as her business would grow, she would be able to travel to different destinations by flight. The train journey had its own charm which she often enjoyed.

A tall, lean man with a black coat and perfectly pressed black jeans called out to Shirin as she was dozing off. He asked Shirin, "Madam, could you please show me your ticket?" with a serious expression on his face.

Shirin handed the ticket to him as she went for her handbag. Tea and snacks were brought out, and she eagerly took out her book, *The Thorn Birds* – a book she enjoyed reading. She became aware of a little spot on her kurta. She tugged on it in order to get a closer look, letting out a disgruntled expression. She had eaten yellow lentil soup earlier in the day, so it was the cause of the spot. She took a deep breath and looked outside the window of the train at undulating hills that gave a picturesque view of the entire terrain.

Shirin appeared to be concerned as she let a notion divert her focus. She had to spend her money extremely carefully because she had taken on a sizable bank loan that she would have to pay back in a year or two. In addition to these other unpaid bills, Kamini and Kiara's school tuition needed to be paid. Shirin recalled that she had informed Babulal of the time and date of her arrival in a message. She was happy that he continued to work for them. The train entered the station with a thud. Shirin's face lit up at the notion of returning home. Hagglers, passengers, beggars, tourists, and residents all crowded into the railway station. On the bench's other side, the heavenly aroma of samosas permeated the thin air. Old, crusty walls of the station were encircled and covered in graffiti and rusted old tracks.

She turned around to see Babulal amid the bustling crowd. He had arrived on time as always. Shirin pushed her way through the crowd as she followed Babulal.

Shirin was being brushed against by a bystander when she abruptly halted and growled at the thug, "Watch out, silly man!"

Babulal made a quick turn and stepped in. "It wouldn't be wise to pick a quarrel with these individuals because it would be late, so let's head to the car, Ma'am."

Shirin was growing restless and impatient to return home as it was now getting dark. She entered the vehicle and exhaled a breath of relief. They had gotten out of the busy city and were on the highway.

In order to breathe some fresh air, she rolled down the automobile window. The lovely breeze blew her silky hair as it stroked her cheeks. It was getting dark and the moon gleamed brightly through the clouds, appearing out of the pitch-black sky sprinkled with stars like a shimmering necklace. The automobile abruptly came to a stop, jerking Shirin forward as it did so.

She asked, afraid and concerned, "What happened, Babulal?"

"Nothing, Madam. Let me go down and inspect the car to make sure everything is okay." He grumbled to himself and whispered under his breath as he scowled. "What might have happened to the vehicle?"

He circled the vehicle to check the tires but thought everything seemed fine.

"I can't figure out what's wrong with the automobile. It's so hard to find a mechanic in the middle of the lonely highway since it's dark now," Babulal said to Shirin with an angry expression on his face.

She appeared distressed and pulled out her phone to see if a mechanic was close by. She googled to check. She bit her lip and had a frightened expression. She exited the car to check if she might get assistance from a bystander.

"Madamji, if you could please sit inside the automobile, I will do something to fix this." After making a few calls, Babulal had an idea and called Rajesh, his younger brother.

"Yes, Bhai, what made you call me at this hour?" asked Rajesh.

Babulal scratched his head and said, "I need help right now. I'm stuck in the middle of the road." Babulal replied after clearing his throat. "I was driving madam's vehicle and suddenly... Hello! Hello! Can you hear me?" Babulal said.

They could hardly talk because of the terrible connectivity. The connection was quickly lost. After randomly looking up a few numbers, he found Vinay's number after clicking his tongue. He dialled his number.

"Hello, Vinay! My madam is with me, and I am in serious trouble. We're stuck in the middle of the road. So, I was wondering if you know any mechanic's number. My attempt to reach the mechanic was unsuccessful because no one answered the phone."

Babulal and Vinay shared the same neighbourhood. Vinay was incredibly helpful by nature and frequently reminded Babulal that he was like his older brother and should never be afraid to ask for assistance. "Let me see if I can help you."

Babulal was antsy and Shirin was becoming increasingly anxious and restless because it had been a while.

"Please roll up your windows and lock your car properly, Madamji. I'll just cross the street and find a mechanic."

Shirin agreed and nodded, but she felt butterflies in her stomach, and her cheeks were flushed from worry. It had been more than an hour. When Shirin peered out of the window, she noticed that the distant, flickering lights of the roadway appeared to be dancing. She was terrified and questioned whether it was okay for her to be in the car in the middle of the road. She opened a small portion of the window to let some fresh air in because she was beginning to feel a little claustrophobic. The rustle of the leaves and the owl's hooting Shirin heard on a nearby tree added to the eerie atmosphere of the night.

Shirin instantly noticed a young well, built man in a black jacket and denim trousers riding a bike and stopping in front of the automobile when she turned her head to the other side.

A handsome man with a strong jawline asked, smiling at her, "Do you need help and support?"

At first, Shirin ignored him and showed no interest in conversing with a stranger.

Shirin declared, "We don't need any assistance from a stranger. My driver has gone to find a mechanic."

Shirin was ignoring him.

She was greeted by the man, who grinned at her. "My name is Vinay, and Babulal just spoke to me. He said your car broke down, and you couldn't find a mechanic." Shirin needed to head back home since it was getting late. He gained her confidence after realised he was the same man Babulal spoke with on the phone a little while ago. She allowed Vinay to check the vehicle.

The man looked at the tires, which all appeared to be in good condition, and then, he looked at the car's bonnet. She made an effort to turn her neck to look at what the stranger was doing. His head was bobbing in her direction. She was unable to see his face properly in the dark. The unknown man sat in the driver's seat and attempted to start the engine. His musky aroma was enticing her senses. Shirin guessed that he was wearing Davidoff cool water, her favourite perfume that she always liked to buy for Arjun once upon a time. She was tempted to see him, Shirin peered in the rear-view mirror to get a glance at him. She noticed a warm feeling close to her heart and had a faint feeling that maybe she had seen him somewhere but she quickly brushed off the thought. Vinay started the automobile and revved the engine in one motion after checking the ignition point. He grinned and said that the spark plug had become loose.

"Phew! It finally functioned. Thank you so much for your help." Shirin replied as she turned to face him in the poor lighting.

"Please don't thank me; I only wanted to help you," Vinay remarked with a smile to Shirin. "I'm glad I could be of assistance." Saying this, Vinay left, and Babulal could be seen, frustrated that he couldn't find a mechanic, walking towards the car from a distance.

"Babulal, you need not be concerned. Vinay, the person you called, came and fixed the issue. The spark plug was loosened." Shirin exhaled a breath of relief as she relaxed in her seat and leaned back.

They eventually arrived home after Babulal started the automobile. Shirin heaved a sigh of relief. She rang the doorbell. Her mother appeared with a smile and flung open the door.

"Oh, my sweetheart, welcome back home! The girls have been waiting for you." Following their embrace, Shirin entered the home and took a deep breath. Returning to one's 'home sweet home' is a wonderful experience.

"Where are the girls? There isn't any noise inside the house."

Babulal entered the house, holding all the things, and handed Shirin a letter. With a startled expression, Shirin pursed her lips and flipped the letter around from all angles to check for an address. When she held the letter up to her nose and smelled the same faint, musky scent of Davidoff that Vinay wore, she felt a chill run down her spine.

I must be incorrect; it's not possible to be true. It can't be him, can it? After furrowing her brows, Shirin carefully opened the letter. With her palm, she attempted to feel the paper's texture. Why is he writing to me? Who is this guy? I'm unsure. It's very mysterious. Shirin bit her lip and decided she didn't want to develop an emotional attachment to any man. No one is still trustworthy to me. I have to look after my family and my company. Kamini and Kiara emerged from their rooms in a rush.

"Mamma, welcome home. Mamma, we are so happy you are home."

Shirin swung up Kiara as she gave them both firm embraces.

"We missed you, Mamma; you are the sweetest!"

This was written on posters that the girls had placed around Shirin's bedroom that night.

Shirin remarked with a big smile, "I am very proud of my girls. You are my true blessings," with wet eyes and quivering lips.

After a relaxing hot shower, Shirin sat down to a satisfying dinner with her family. Her mother had prepared her favourite *bhindi sabzi* and *rajma* for her.

"Eating homemade food is the best treatment for the tummy; nothing can replace it."

Shirin wanted to call it a day because she was exhausted, and it was late at night. Shirin retired to her room and regretted not spending the day in bed. She tossed and turned in the guest house bed all night because the mattress's musty odour was overpowering. When Shirin reached for the bedside lamp to turn off the light, she unexpectedly noticed the envelope that Babulal had given her.

She had a notion when she was holding the letter. When the stranger helped her, she grinned as memories of the incident returned. She tried to remember his facial features but found it difficult to recall because it was dark and his face wasn't particularly distinct. This time, Shirin smiled and questioned herself as she opened the letter. Am I harbouring a secret affection for the anonymous writer who has been writing to me regularly? She found a lot of solace and security in these letters. After reading the letter, Shirin tore it open because she couldn't wait any longer.

"Your path throughout life might not be a pleasant one.

But remember, only cowards opt for the simple solution.

You are an unstoppable fighter.

So, nothing can stop you from achieving your most cherished dreams.

Just believe in your limitless strength and wisdom."

Chapter 14
A Success Story

Shirin looked stunning in a handcrafted ethnic salwar suit made of *tussar* silk that Zulfikar, the leader of the Warangal weavers, had specially woven for Shirin on her 45th birthday. Today was a momentous day for Shirin since she had an interview with Business Hub, a renowned business publication.

She earned her spot on the magazine's cover with a lot of hard work and was nominated as the most successful business entrepreneur in the apparel industry for the current year. She was ready to share her success story on how she had overcome the numerous obstacles she had to confront in her long and arduous journey.

The intercom rang loud startling Shirin who was looking at some important official documents.

Shirin took out her phone and said, "Yes, tell me."

"Business Hub's reporter, Ms Reema is here to meet you," said Rani, Shirin's secretary who spoke in a raspy voice. She was a petite little girl with a smiling face and gleaming eyes, always in a happy mood.

Shirin had a well-designed, roomy office in an upscale city neighbourhood. After a modest beginning, Spindle Wheels Pvt. Ltd. had grown into a thriving textile business in just ten years.

Shirin began with a 2-lakh rupee investment, and throughout the years, the investment paid off as sales increased to 4 crore rupees with a significant turnover. Shirin readjusted the crease in her silk dupatta when she heard a tap at the door.

"The door is open, come in," Shirin spoke in a loud, clear voice.

Reema smiled at Shirin as she introduced herself and entered the office cabin, her shoes making a little thudding sound on the hard wooden floor. Reema was a lovely young lady with deep brown eyes that were slightly dreamy yet so finely placed beneath arched brows, complemented by a long, pointed nose and well-curved lips. Shirin adjusted the position of her chair and straightened her back.

Shirin was overcome with happiness at being picked among numerous others by well-known magazine publishers. She had put in a lot of effort to reach this level of accomplishment.

Leaning forward from her chair, Reema pulled out a notebook and her list of questions for the interview.

"Ma'am," Reema asked with a glint in her eyes, "Are you ready, Shirin ma'am, for some direct questions?"

"Shoot out, I'm ready," Shirin responded, lifting her chin with assurance.

While recording the notes, Shirin saw that Reema was donning a vintage HMT wristwatch with tattered leather straps.

Shirin pondered why she was still sporting an outmoded timepiece at a time when the younger generation preferred smartwatches.

Shirin recounted her inspiring tale of growing Spindle Wheels Pvt. Ltd. from a modest manufacturing facility in her garage to a fully operational business.

Shirin answered Reema's question, "How have you progressed as a person in your work?"

Shirin smiled and said that she made a good profit but never at the cost of taking advantage of the benefits and profit of the poor weavers who worked very hard with honesty. This point was thought-provoking. The interview lasted an hour and featured many more insightful topics and questions.

After pausing for a few seconds, Shirin exhaled deeply before responding, "When I first started my business enterprise, I experienced several hurdles. I had no one to turn to for advice or support, and there were times when I considered giving up when faced with the toughest barriers. Still, I persisted because I knew I had to set an example for my two precious daughters by working hard to fulfil my dreams of becoming a successful businesswoman and never giving up in the face of challenges."

In an enthusiastic tone, Reema asked her about the NGO Shirin had started for the Warangal weavers' children.

"Could you perhaps explain the rationale for founding the NGO in Warangal for the disadvantaged mothers and children?"

With shining eyes, Shirin addressed Reema while in a reflective state. "I've always wanted to contribute to society in some way, and I was particularly moved to create a school in Warangal for the underprivileged children of weavers."

Shirin smiled saying, "I frequently travelled to the villages for work. I witnessed the miserable living conditions of the weavers, who, despite their desire to educate their children, couldn't afford to send their children to school. I decided to do something for them. I considered starting a school for the benefit of the kids. Even women wanted to enrol in night classes and acquire a basic education."

"In today's world, a businessman would simply want to earn a profit at the expense of cheap labour here; you are thinking about the welfare of the poor weavers."

Shirin stood up from her chair to shake Reema's hand after the interview. Reema shook Shirin's hand and smiled, expressing gratitude for her time.

The cameraman who had been with her was waiting at the front desk when Reema sent Nagesh a message telling him to head over to Shirin's office.

A tall, lanky man with a dark complexion entered Shirin's workplace carrying a digital camera and sporting a ponytail with a hunch. As a senior cinematographer, Nagesh, introduced himself and asked Shirin if he could take a few shots of her for the interview.

"I am not the type of person who is at ease during photo shoots. So, please keep it brief and quick," Shirin remarked as she nodded.

Shirin noticed that Nagesh photographed Shirin several times from various angles for the magazine cover page.

"Thank you for your time," Reema replied as she glanced at the clock.

"Can I ask you something?" Shirin asked, turning to face Reema.

Reema was mildly surprised and pondered what Shirin may want to ask her.

Sure, Reema replied, raising her chin.

"I thought of asking you…it's intriguing to see an old HMT watch on your wrist, something one wouldn't see in the present age," Shirin said diplomatically.

Reema rolled up her shirt sleeves, adjusted her watch, and raised her wrists to get a better look at her watch. "Well, my mother, who passed away from cancer while I was in grade 9, owned this watch." Tears welled up in Reema's eyes, and she looked down at her watch.

"I am sorry to hear that", Shirin remarked as she inched closer to Reema and placed her hand on her shoulder.

Reema smiled at Shirin and said," I'm glad you spotted my watch. People at work occasionally smirk at me and think it's not trendy to wear this outdated watch, but who cares. What others think doesn't really worry me."

***

The birds on the balcony were singing, and the sun was just beginning to break through the morning clouds. A pleasant aroma of jasmine and fresh-cut grass floated in the humid summer air. The jingling of the wind chime was soothing to the ears as it swayed and danced in the breeze. Shirin sat down with a cup of ginger-flavoured hot tea after her morning ritual of feeding the sparrows.

Shirin saw Kiara skip out of the living room and onto the balcony. "Mamma, I am ready to leave for college, and how is my new pink top looking?" she asked.

Shirin looked up at Kiara with a grin on her face. Kiara had on a lovely pink floral top and skinny jeans. Shirin's daughters had worked very hard in school, and she was very proud of them.

Kiara was in her second year at a prestigious university, studying software engineering. Kamini had graduated with a Master of Science in Business Administration from a similarly prestigious institution, also on a full scholarship.

Shirin kissed her forehead; she embraced Kiara and gushed, "You always look beautiful in all your dresses, my darling."

After hugging Shirin, Kiara said, "I miss Kamini Didi so much; can't she come home from her business trip quickly?"

Shirin smiled and said to Kiara, "She will be home next week, my love."

Kamini had to fly all the way to Mumbai to sign this contract. It was a big deal for the company. Also, she will have to stay in Mumbai for a month to start the new office in Mumbai.

Shirin smiled at Kiara and said, "By the way, when your sister gets together, you always argue, and when she's gone, you miss Kamini."

Kiara shrugged and grabbed her backpack, ready to head off to college. "I love you, Mom. I'll see you later today."

Shirin went to the garden and sat on her favourite garden chair after Kiara left. When Shirin heard the rusty old wind chime, she was taken back to the days when her daughters, Kiara and Kamini, played with their doll houses in the garden. At the same time, she ate her breakfast, sometimes joined by Arjun if he was home on a Sunday, under the garden umbrella. Since she had always wanted a lemon tree in her garden, Roshani specifically brought her Avalon lemon tree saplings. Shirin's sister Roshani gifted her several Avalon lemon tree saplings that she tended to with great care over the years.

A tiny sapling grows into a mighty tree that can survive both freezing temperatures in winter and searing heat in the summer.

It is impervious to the wrath of the storms and stands firm through them all.

Instead, it strengthens its roots to the ground with each blow of a storm.

The tree's leaves always sport a new ensemble, whether fall or spring.

Mankind, like a tree, must remain unmoved by the vicissitudes of life, just as the tree stands firm through all four seasons.

Chapter 15
Shadows from the Past

Babulal was taking Shirin to work through rush hour at 9:30 a.m. It was chaos on a busy Monday morning. The street was bustling with activity, and the screaming traffic horns added to the noise of the traffic jam.

Babulal grumbled as he shifted gears, "The traffic on this route has worsened over the years. Fifteen years ago, there was no traffic on this road, and the skyline over the horizon was clean and bright; now, with the mushrooming of so many shops and offices, there is just a concrete jungle around us."

While using her laptop to check her emails, Shirin continued nodding in accord with Babulal.

While looking in the rear-view mirror, Babulal attempted to reposition it. "Madamji, driving in this frenzied traffic is challenging. Next year, I either want to retire or take a long leave of absence. My older son, Sharad, employed by a reputable MNC, frequently advises me to return to the village and live a tranquil life in retirement."

"You have worked very hard your entire life. So, I think it will be a good idea to take a break and rest for some time," Shirin remarked as she briefly looked up and adjusted her reading glasses.

In anticipation of the day's key meetings and interviews, particularly those pertaining to the new office that Kamini was handling, Shirin arrived at her workplace.

"There is something special kept for you on your table, Madam," Rani, Shirin's secretary, announced as she rose up to greet Shirin. Shirin's mind was wandering and she was constantly thinking about the new office in Mumbai that was being looked after by Kamini. She stepped into her cabin without paying much attention to Rani who was busy doing her work on the laptop.

Shirin glanced at her table and was thrilled to see the first copy of "Business Hub magazine" with her beautiful photo on the cover page. Shirin was overcome with delight at the time and couldn't believe that this was for real. Her happiness knew no boundaries as she appeared on the cover of the special issue of a prestigious business magazine.

Shirin removed the drawer from her desk and inspected the collection of letters she had amassed over time. She blushed as she caressed the letters and sifted through them with her fingertips.

'Who is this stranger who has helped me every time I've faced adversity? His writings have inspired me so much, and I treasure the strong desire to see him someday. Is he present in this city or another? Where could he be?' Shirin grinned as she stroked her cheeks and clasped the letters in her palms.

Shirin became preoccupied due to her phone's continuous notifications. She beamed as she started to receive numerous texts from friends and family congratulating her, including Kamini, Kiara, Roshani, her mother, her dear friend Meenakshi and many other friends.

As Shirin was enjoying herself, her phone abruptly rang while she was checking her messages.

Shirin furrowed her brows in anticipation of the caller.

Roshani was on the line. "Congratulations, my beloved sister; you are a successful businesswoman and a celebrity. This amazing moment deserves a toast; therefore, let's do that. Your favourite mountain location is the perfect destination where you will celebrate your 50th birthday this year."

"Didi, I would want to go to Mukteshwar this time on my birthday," Shirin interjected.

Roshani remarked right away, "No way, let's arrange a vacation into the beautiful highlands of Scotland; it's the ideal gorgeous location for your birthday. Your birthday is going to be a special celebration and more so because it's your 50th."

"That will be the perfect birthday celebration," Shirin smiled and said. "I'll call Meenakshi my darling friend from Bangalore as well. We used to hang out all the time in college, but once she got married, we hardly ever had the chance to meet often."

At Roshani's end, the internet connection appeared to be spotty.

When the call abruptly disconnected, Shirin checked her mobile device. The landline started ringing. Shirin answered the call and it was Roshani Didi on line, "What happened to your phone?" While Shirin was talking, Rani interrupted and said, "A gentleman named Arjun is waiting to see you at the reception."

For a moment, Shirin was immobile and unable to respond.

Roshani called out on the phone from the other end, "What happened, Shirin? Why are you suddenly so quiet?"

Shirin couldn't react to what she just heard and said, "I don't believe this, it's not possible."

Roshani, who was still online and had overheard Shirin, asked, "Are you okay, Shirin? What happened to you?"

"Didi, I will call you back," Shirin fumbled on the phone and quickly hung up.

"Arjun? No, it cannot be him." Shirin looked worried. "No, it's not possible after so many years. It has to be someone else." Shirin suddenly dropped to the ground, hitting her chair with a loud thud as her hands started to shake with panic. Shirin thought she could no longer feel the earth.

Hearing all the noise, Rani came running.

"Ma'am, are you okay?" Rani worriedly asked Shirin.

"Can I do something?" Rani got Shirin a glass of water. Shirin waved her hand, wanting to be left alone.

"I'm fine, let me be for some time, please." Shirin put her head back. "Send the visitor to my cabin, please."

Rani looked astonished since she had never seen Shirin in such a mood. Rani looked surprised and shrugged her shoulders.

There was a knock on Shirin's cabin door. Shirin moved in her chair and responded, "Yes, come in."

"Shirin, congratulations!" Arjun replied in a weak voice, "You have accomplished enormous success in such a short time."

"Where have you been all these years?" Shirin demanded in a harsh voice. And suddenly, you have emerged after so many years."

Shirin experienced numbness as all of her memories of Arjun resurfaced. After clearing his throat, Arjun apologised for all the suffering he had caused.

"Please accept my sincere request for pardon." Arjun stood there sheepishly, looking very guilty. "After I unexpectedly left all of you and faced bankruptcy, I did not dare to face you or my daughters."

Shirin's eyes flooded with tears, but she balanced her rage. "Arjun, you always had your way with things, and I could never make important house decisions without your permission, but after you left us at a crossroads, after years of struggle and overcoming many challenges, I have emerged stronger, and I no longer need you in my life," she grinned at Arjun. "For so many years, you haven't bothered to ask about my daughters or me despite the fact that I have supported them solely." With anger in her voice, Shirin said, "You acted cowardly by doing that. When I first tried to reach you, you were inaccessible, as if you had disappeared into thin air. Now you have come all the way here to congratulate me after learning about the success of my company through my interview in the Hub Magazine."

Shirin gritted her teeth and moved closer to Arjun. "All of this was made possible by my labour, sweat, and blood."

With great regret, Arjun admitted, "I had relocated to Bologna, Italy, and joined Vestiti Galvani for a while to avoid the creditors chasing me to pay off the loans. I was unable to provide you with my location. I decided to stay there and never considered returning to India. I am guilty of what I did to you and the girls and I don't expect your forgiveness. I was in town on business, and tomorrow night's flight will take me away."

Shirin was fuming with rage, "You have been very selfish, Arjun, leaving all the responsibility of the company on me. I had no clue where to start and where to end. I was at crossroads wondering which direction to choose, but I can proudly say that I made the correct choices in life and with my dedication and hard work I have accomplished my dream."

Meanwhile, Arjun's mobile started ringing.

"Ciao, Cara!" said Arjun in Italian.

Shirin heard a woman speaking in Italian to Arjun. Arjun smiled as he was talking on the phone and Shirin could make out that this wasn't a business call.

Shirin tried to look from the corner of her eyes. Arjun attempted to muffle the sound by placing his hand on the phone's speaker, but it was ineffective. Shirin sat on her chair, reclined her head, fixed her eyes on the ceiling, and inhaled deeply.

"So, your wife is Italian?"

"Allow me to clarify this," Arjun replied as he sent a direct glance at Shirin's way.

"The well-known clothing shop that Aria's father owned needed management because he was ill and Aria, my wife, was dealing with numerous health difficulties. I had to comfort and reassure Aria's father in some way."

Shirin smiled wryly and said, "You saw your advantage and looking at their solid financial history, you must have thought that you could start a new chapter of your life." Shirin looked at Arjun sternly.

Shirin shook her head angrily while feeling extremely annoyed.

"I'm sorry, Arjun; this is too much for a day to handle; kindly leave me alone for the time being."

Arjun was surprised because he had never noticed Shirin being so straight and harsh before.

"I am content with my daughters in my tiny world," Shirin replied as she stared into his eyes. "I desire to lead a tranquil and contented life. I don't want the sacredness of my home to be disturbed by any hurtful memories from the past."

Shirin turned and glared scornfully in the direction of the entrance.

Arjun stood up, made no comment, and left Shirin's cabin.

With a lump in her throat, Shirin pursed her lips and peered out her cabin window. Shirin believed Arjun had betrayed her and questioned why he had not gotten in touch with them for so long.

'*I waited for so many years, wondering where he was and hoping he wasn't having any problems while single-mindedly raising my two girls on my own.*'

Shirin heard a knock on the door. Miss Archana, the head of the HR department, walked in.

After taking a deep breath, Shirin reclined in her chair. "Yes, kindly enter."

The 28-year-old Archana was a tall, well-built woman with long, cascading chestnut brown hair, a beaming smile, and dazzling eyes. With her pen in hand, Archana began to check down the names of those she had spoken with and who had been chosen for the Mumbai office. Shirin found it difficult to focus on what Archana was saying. After meeting Arjun, she was in utter shock and disbelief.

Shirin was approached by Archana, who asked, "Ma'am, are you okay? You are sweating even with air conditioning."

"I'm alright," said Shirin with a wave of her hand. "You may proceed."

"I have emailed the official documents to Kamini Madam," Archana told Shirin.

Shirin's preoccupied appearance made it difficult for her to concentrate on what Archana was saying.

Suddenly, her phone rang. It was Kamini on the line, and she sounded very nervous.

"Mom, Mom, there has been an accident," she said, sounding incredibly terrified and concerned. "Accidentally, one of the guards on duty last night in the warehouse got shot by a few goons when he was on night duty and injured his leg in the scuffle. Another guard managed to inform the police on time. The cops reached here on time, but there is a lot of stress and mess to be handled here." Kamini sounded very worried.

Shirin instructed her secretary to arrange her travel to Mumbai as soon as possible.

There had been just too much happening in a single day.

The celebration of her accomplishment on the magazine cover had kicked off the day, but when she met Arjun, it was a startling turn of events that sent shivers down her spine. Kamini's panic call added to her day's tension as it ended.

Babulal drove Shirin to the airport. From the window of her automobile, Shirin could observe the sun lowering over the horizon.

Birds were swarming back to their nests as the sun's colours painted the sky a soft, warm orange tone. One day has seen a lot of activity. Despite the several upheavals, she recalled what she had read in his most recent letter, and the passage was ingrained in her memory.

"A new dawn is promised with every sunset.

Nothing stays forever and everything is in a constant state of flux.

What matters is moving ahead with a strong will

and not getting swayed by the challenges that life throws at us."

Chapter 16

Monsoon Season in Mumbai

After a late evening flight, Shirin collected her bags at the Mumbai airport and reached Exit Gate number 2. She stuck her head out into the crowd to see if Rajkumar, the office peon who was supposed to meet her at the airport on behalf of Kamini, was there.

Even though Shirin would have appreciated it, Kamini's text that she was out bar hopping with her best friend and would be home late left her disappointed. After a while, the chaos of the office became too much for Kamini, and she texted Shirin that she had to go out because she needed a break.

Rajkumar spotted Shirin amongst the crowd and beckoned for her to follow, saying, "Madam, please come this way; welcome to Mumbai."

Rajkumar, a short, lanky young man with a bright grin and well-combed hair, picked up Shirin's bags and headed for the car. The streets were slushy, and puddles could be found just about anywhere because of the light rain.

Rajkumar readjusted his coat and offered Shirin an umbrella as it began to rain.

"Madam, the rains in Mumbai can sometimes be destructive and persistent. If it rains heavily during the monsoon season, the city can come to a grinding halt."

Not paying close attention to the chaperone's words, Shirin ignored what she was told to do. More than anything else, she was anxious to get to the warehouse and see how bad the accident had been there.

Shirin furrowed her brows in worry and reached for her phone, calling her daughter, Kamini.

Kamini finally answered her call after a while. "My darling, where have you been?"

"Mamma, I told you my best friend Mishika has come from Singapore; I am out with her," was Kamini's hasty response. "Guddi Bai will be available to prepare and serve dinner even though I'll arrive late. I will catch up with you in the morning."

Shirin was annoyed by Kamini's behaviour and said, "I am coming to meet you after such a long time and was hoping to see you at the airport. I hope the injured security guard is doing well and that he and his family have been compensated fairly for their loss?"

Kamini had to shout over the music that was playing very loudly in the background.

"Mom, you can rest easy because our company's lawyer, Mr S. K. Sharma, handles everything."

Serious in her tone, Shirin said, "I am more concerned about the safety of the security guard, who did his duty diligently. God bless him and his loved ones."

Shirin strolled into Kamini's tastefully furnished apartment and took a look around. It was a clean and comfortable apartment that exuded a pleasant vibe. Shirin felt at ease in the drawing room, thanks to the floral wallpaper and the scent of the French vanilla candles.

Her daughter maintaining such a lovely and orderly home brought her much joy. The isolation brought on Shirin's nightmares. She felt at home. Shirin knew she would feel lonely and homesick upon her return to Bangalore. She longed to confide in someone and have them share her joy and laughter. For what felt like an eternity, she longed to finally meet her secret lover.

Due to exhaustion, Shirin retired to Kamini's bedroom. She continued reading the novel she had brought along on the plane, and Shirin reached into her purse. She looked over at the side table and saw a picture frame. She picked it up to observe it more closely; the picture was an old family snapshot of Arjun, Kamini, Kiara, and Shirin, the latter of whom was perched on the branch of a tree, her hair falling loosely around her.

When Shirin saw the photo, she smiled and felt the rage towards Arjun begin to subside. She'd forgiven him, she knew, and the quest for her stranger made Shirin blush with happiness. Exactly where could he be at this moment? The desire to finally meet him was something she harboured in secret.

If he really cares about me, he'll make an effort to write to me, and this time, we'll definitely meet. The next morning, Shirin woke up early and reached the warehouse where the accident had occurred.

The warehouse got a whiff of floral-scented sweetness as Shirin, dressed in a crisp cotton saree, walked in. Mr Sharad, the manager, walked around in his business suit nervously.

"I hope the guard is okay, Mr Sharad, I heard he was seriously hurt."

Mr Sharad smiled and nodded his agreement, saying, "Madam, we have compensated for all his losses; money makes all the difference; it's been taken care of."

With a frown and an angry look, Shirin said, "I am more concerned about his recovery than the money. Money must be everything for you, but it's not for me."

Shirin tapped her fingers on the table, looked the manager in the eye, and said, "I will skirt the entire complex and take a good look at the warehouse to ensure that the safety measures are in place."

Kamini entered her cabin in a beautiful cotton jacket and pants.

Kamini told her mother, "Mamma, I am so happy to see you. Sorry, I wasn't there last night with you."

Shirin smiled and said, "It's fine, my darling."

Kamini showed irritation and said asked why did this happen despite all the precautionary measures being taken in the factory and the efforts being put in.

Shirin looked at Kamini and said, "You cannot give up so easily, have patience. Remember, the two wheels of a cart, honesty and hard work, go hand in hand and will always propel you forward towards your goal if you persist."

Kamini beamed, her eyes bright, and said, "You can trust me, Mom; I just got a little nervous after the accident."

Shirin looked at Kamini and said, "You have to be strong, my dear, and be ready to face the unexpected situations that life suddenly throws at us. Wisdom and fortitude to deal with life's difficulties will come to you as you practise patience and resilience over time."

Shirin approached Kamini, put her hands on her shoulders, and declared, "I entrust you and Kiara with the entire responsibility of Spindle Wheels Pvt. Ltd. I'm ready to resign and travel the world. I want to retire now. I've put a lot of effort into building this empire, and it's literally paid off in the form of blood and sweat. This time, it's up to you to shoulder the responsibility. My daughters are accomplished professionals who can lead Spindle to new heights."

While Shirin was in the office, the manager of human resources, Raveena, entered the cabin carrying a black file. Raveena had long, lustrous hair and a curvy, average-sized frame.

She entered the cabin with a solemn expression, despite being by nature a vivacious young woman.

She greeted Shirin and Kamini with a warm smile and informed Kamini, "Kamini Ma'am, the guy, Vinay, who was fired by Sharad Sir yesterday is absolutely innocent and it wasn't his fault at all."

Shirin felt her heart skip a beat and froze for a second. "Vinay, I think I have heard that name before."

Kamini looked at her mother from the corner of her eye and asked, "Mamma, how do you know Vinay?"

Shirin pursed her lips and did not know what to tell Kamini.

Raveena continued in a hushed tone, "It is the supervisor, Sharad, who misplaced the file and passed on our precious official data to our rival company, Cotton India. He received a bribe of two lakh rupees for doing that. Since Mr Sharad was never very tech-savvy, it's good that the IT director was able to salvage the official document before Sharad could have hidden the file somewhere."

Shirin's mind flashed on a familiar name, and she got out of her chair to ask, "Where is this guy, Vinay?"

"If he has worked in this office, why haven't I heard of him? And why wasn't I told about him joining the Mumbai office?" Kamini looked surprised and wondered why did her mother say so.

Before the accident and the file's disappearance, Kamini had assured Shirin that she could handle the situation independently.

Raveena turned to Shirin and said, "Madam, Vinay was a very sincere and hard-working man who worked extremely hard for the company's growth. When Kamini Ma'am took over the Mumbai office a year ago, he was transferred from Bangalore to work with us. He greatly helped boost business in Western India."

With a serious expression, Kamini said, "Now I know why Sharad always found reasons to blame Vinay for any problem related to sales and marketing."

This time, Sharad was right on the money, pinning the loss of a file containing the personal mobile numbers of every CEO of a global brand on that single factor.

Shirin stood by the window as night fell, peering out at the moonlight filtering through the trees.

A violent storm woke Shirin up, and she realised this must be a sign that she couldn't afford to miss the chance to discover where Vinay had disappeared.

Chapter 17
The Quest

Shirin was awakened from her sleep by the noise of the singing sparrows in the garden on this bright, beautiful day. Her cheeks warmed as the sun poured in through the window. She had a memorable day because it was her 50th birthday. The previous morning, Kiara had come from Pennsylvania. She wanted to surprise Shirin and quickly sneaked into the room, planning to surprise Shirin. She was finishing her Executive MBA at the University of Pennsylvania and wished to settle there. For Shirin's special birthday, Kiara and Kamini had prepared several surprises. Even though Shirin was having a great time, she couldn't help but be distracted and wished to see Vinay. Vinay had been unfairly accused of something he was never responsible for, and Shirin felt terrible about that.

"Mamma, we have arranged a wonderful vacation to Scotland, and it would be a dream come true," Kiara and Kamini told Shirin as they hugged her. "Roshani Masi and Tuli Aunty have been invited for a nice vacation around your birthday."

"Why do you want to spend money, my lovely girls?" Shirin asked with a smile.

In unison, Kiara and Kamini said, "Oh!" as they exchanged glances. "Enjoy life and have some fun, Mother; come on!"

Shirin felt the temptation; of course, she had long dreamed of taking a girlie vacation to Scotland. Perhaps, this was the ideal time.

"Mamma, you know I aim to settle in the US. I would absolutely want you and Kamini to frequently come to the US—that is, if she wants to see me," Kiara added sarcastically, glancing at Kamini.

Kiara placed her hands on Shirin's shoulders. As she looked at Kiara, Kamini lifted her face up. Shirin didn't listen to what the girls were saying.

"You don't seem to be paying much attention to what we are saying, Mamma," Kamini asked Shirin. "Are you feeling well?"

Shirin smiled while raising her eyebrows as she turned to face Kamini. "On my special birthday, Roshani Masi, Tuli Aunty, and I would love to travel to Scotland. But I have been wondering where Vinay went. The way he left it wasn't fair in the least. This has been unfair on our part."

Kiara shrugged as she looked at Shirin.

"It's irrelevant. He'll come up with a solution on his own. Mamma, why do you seem bothered?"

Shirin made the driver available because she wasn't persuaded. "Girls, I'll retrieve a file I need from the office immediately. I'll return in 20 minutes." Kamini and Kiara were conversing and checking their messages while using their phones.

While texting, Kiara stated, "Mama, you need to relax today."

Kamini walked to her room and got into her favourite outfit. Shirin noticed Kamini arranging her makeup on the dresser as she entered her room because Kamini had left the door open.

"Are you going anywhere, beta?" Shirin stepped into Kamini's room while furrowing her brows.

Kamini said, "Oh, yes!" while talking on the phone and appeared disoriented.

"I thought we could have a family lunch together, and then I could catch up with my friends in the evening. In fact, Rishabh, my friend from my college I had mentioned and his dear friend has arrived from London for a few days, and we intended to meet in the evening."

Shirin didn't look very happy and expected that because it was her 50th birthday, she should be going out for a special dinner with Kamini. Although Shirin wanted to spend the whole day with her girls, she questioned whether she wasn't asking too much of them.

While getting into the car, Shirin spotted a stunning bouquet of pink roses next to her mailbox. She grinned while blushing slightly and arching her brows. She was now aware that her elusive, hidden admirer had written this letter. As she took the letter and pressed it against her chest, Shirin grinned. Her cheeks turned pink from the warmth. Although she longed to read the letter, she carefully placed it in her purse instead. She sat down in her car, carefully took the letter out, and started to read.

"My sweetheart,

Upon your memorable 50ᵗʰ birthday, as you begin a new chapter in your life, for all your efforts and accomplishments, I admire you.

You've had a difficult journey but have courageously taken every step.

Take pride in your accomplishments and have faith in your boundless potential.

You have diligently performed your maternal responsibilities.

Live a life that appeals to you and search for your true companion, who is waiting for you across the ocean.

My heart longs for the warmth of your love, and like the way the river merges with the ocean, so will our hearts soon unite.

In order to demonstrate the purity and strength of my love for you, I hope that we will come together just like true lovers. Over the far horizon, I'll be watching for you. This is my last letter to you.

Despite my best efforts to assist Kamini in opening the Mumbai office, it crushed my heart when I was falsely accused of falsifying reports. I'm glad I was able to shield Kamini from Mr Sharad's wrongdoings because he had every intention of damaging the business and attempting an aggressive takeover.

Vinay, your ardent admirer"

With tears in her eyes, Shirin was eager to get to her office. She went to her cabin as soon as she entered the workplace because she was restless. Shirin's birthday song was sung in the office while everyone stood up and joined in throughout.

Everyone wanted to help her celebrate her birthday, but she moved aside, raced to her cabin, and apologised, saying, "I am so sorry; I have other plans, so I will be going shortly."

In an effort to locate his address, she yanked out her drawer and began hurriedly sorting through all the envelopes from the letters she had already received. She did as she always did and calculated the total number of letters. She realised this was Vinay's 17th letter and got the shivers. She was so far away from him, even though he was so close. She realised how close they were and how he had always written to her to support her and show his profound love for her. Throughout all of this time, however, she had been unaware of the depth of his love. Bracing herself, Shirin summoned her confidence and asked the HR manager.

Raveena wished Shirin and gave her a huge bouquet of roses, "Happy birthday to Shirin Ma'am," she said while grinning and saying, "Ma'am, you called for me."

Shirin asked, "I want Vinay's home address right now," as she turned to face her with a serious expression.

"But, ma'am, he has already left; is everything all right?" Raveena asked while nodding.

"There are no questions, please provide his mailing address. It is urgent," Shirin glared at her.

Raveena left for her cabin and came back holding a document. "This is Vinay's resume, Ma'am, and it contains his mailing address."

Shirin stood up from her seat, took the file, and hurriedly left her cabin. Vinay relocated to Bangalore many years back from Mumbai after learning of Arjun's mysterious disappearance. He was in close touch with Babulal, the driver and had befriended him to keep track of Shirin. Shirin and Vinay went to the same school from elementary to high school. Vinay was barely six years old when his father passed away, leaving him to live with his mother. His mother was the sole breadwinner of the family, he understood her struggles and put in a lot of effort and eventually earned his engineering degree in software from a reputable college. Since he was in school, Vinay secretly admired Shirin and vowed in his heart to marry her and no one else. He did attempt to propose to her in school in grade 9 but Shirin never showed interest and frequently thought of him as just another random classmate. Vinay was always hoping for an opportunity to spend the rest of his life with Shirin. Would she ever develop feelings for him?

The following morning, Shirin was dressed in her favourite lemon-coloured suit and a white dupatta with intricate embroidery. She was worried about the trip and had butterflies in her stomach. When her phone started to ring, she peered at the screen to see Roshani on the other end of the line. When Shirin finally answered the call, she did so unwillingly and greeted Roshani Didi. She was aware that Roshani was looking forward to their trip to Scotland.

"I can't wait to get there, and my schedule is all set," Roshani remarked.

"We're going to have a great time. Didi, please don't be unhappy, but can we postpone the vacation as I urgently need to go to Warangal?" Shirin was hesitant to tell her older sister this, but she eventually found the strength to say it.

Astounded, Roshani literally screamed, "Shirin, are you even aware of what you are saying? You've got to be crazy. How can you destroy our programme on your 50th birthday? What has happened to you?"

"Didi, please don't stop me; I am going to Warangal to make the most crucial decision of my life," breathed Shirin after taking a long breath. "Either now or never."

"Where are Kiara and Kamini?" Roshani inquired with a subdued voice.

Shirin raised an eyebrow and shook her shoulders.

"They had gone out with their buddies last night, so I presume they had their own independent life. Didi, I've got to hang up, and I promise I'll return home to see you soon, but for now, I have to go," replied Shirin hastily.

Shirin was expecting Chotelal, her new driver, to pick her up and take her to the train station, but Babulal actually arrived to pick her up.

"Babulal, I didn't expect to see you here," Shirin replied with an astonished expression on her face. "I mistook you for returning to your hometown."

"Madamji, I received a message from Vinay, who said that he needed a special favour from me and if I could drop you off at the railway station like old times," Shirin recalled that night and furrowed her brows questioning Babulal. "So, tell me all about it, how well do you know Vinay?"

With a wrinkly, bespectacled face and a smile, Babulal stated to Shirin, "Vinay resided in the neighbourhood around my home for more than ten years; Vinay would often ask me about you and your daughters. Years ago, when I picked you up from the station and our car broke down in the middle of a deserted area, a stranger helped us. I later discovered that the person who had assisted us was Vinay, my neighbour. He is a good man who always helps everyone in the neighbourhood. He was very popular in our locality. He always had the solution for every problem."

Shirin was growing restless as she grew impatient to board the train and travel to Warangal. Shirin arrived in Warangal and noticed the dusty town and the animals on the highway. She took a glance at the address before entering the lane. The cold breeze caressed her from the paddy fields as it got later in the day. After taking a deep breath, Shirin felt at ease thanks to the fields' enticing aroma. She found the birds chirping to be music to her ears, and it helped calm and relax her. It provided relief from the mundane routine of city life. Shirin was experiencing conflicting emotions and feelings. She flushed and pondered her next question for Vinay. She entered the alleyways that led to a large, verdant field filled with vibrant sunflowers. It was breathtaking to see the sunflower fields decorated with vibrant tones of yellow and brown and the sea of blue that covered the sky. A school for kids and adults was located across the area. It was a bustling place with a happy vibe.

Shirin observed the peace and simplicity of the scene while standing still. Vinay was the person she wanted to meet, and when she looked at the résumé and saw his home address, she knew she was in the right place. Despite the chaos, she could hear his footsteps and felt a man's fingers warmly touch her shoulders. She recognised the same musky body odour as its owner since she could smell it. She whirled around to look at him.

A strikingly chiselled young man in his fifties with a gorgeous face. When she eventually turned to face Vinay, she asked him, "Why did you come back? Why couldn't we get together sooner? I yearned to meet you and anxiously searched for you everywhere, but you had vanished. Why?"

"I had originally proposed to you in school when you were in grade 9, but you mocked me and stated that you would marry a guy who would prove his love and could reveal the depth of his devotion," Vinay said while holding her hand. "I was in love with you ever since I saw you for the first time in school in grade eight," Vinay commented, his eyes growing intensely. "I had already decided that you would be the only person I would marry if I ever did. I even proposed to you in college, but I assume you had already decided to marry Arjun."

Shirin struggled to control the tears that were streaming down her cheeks. Shirin was made to sit down on a wooden seat by Vinay when he drew nearer and put his hands on her shoulders. Vinay chuckled as he said, "I made a commitment to win your affection and demonstrate my love for you, and I've succeeded in realising my dream of marrying the person I fell in love with the first time we met in school. You are my true soulmate, and I will wait for you forever; I have made up my mind."

Shirin felt a warm wave of affection and excitement rush down her spine as he drew closer and raised her chin.

Vinay remarked, "I chose to work at your Mumbai office so that I could help your firm produce a profit while still being able to protect you and Kamini," as he fixed an intense glare on Shirin.

"I occasionally wrote to you because I could tell how difficult it was for you to start your own business and how hard it was for you to give your daughters a good education. I have eagerly waited for you to fulfil your duties as a mother."

Shirin looked at Vinay and wondered, '*How could* anyone *love me so sincerely and unconditionally? Is this true and pure love?*'

Vinay looked into her eyes and said, "You have undergone a remarkable transformation from a timid and reserved young girl to a powerful and independent lady."

Shirin grinned and informed Vinay that he had been watching her all along. Vinay gripped Shirin's hand while they exchanged glances, adding, "Do you see these kids over here? They are orphans, and I have been caring for them, providing for their education, and offering practical courses to help these kids become independent. We also provide classes for people who want to further their education. I have been the sole source of finance for this school for the villages because I want them to someday integrate into society."

Shirin tried to recall all the letters that Vinay had written to Shirin. Vinay had opened a school in memory of his deceased mother and father. Children from the local villages came to study here. Vinay, after the incident in the Mumbai office, decided to shift permanently to his village in Lingagiri. There was absolute peace and serenity in the village here. Vinay had happily settled down here. He had undertaken a lot of corporate assignments that he could deliver and most of his work was online.

Shirin was aware of her next course of action. Shirin phoned Roshani.

She picked up the phone and sounded enthusiastic about their Scotland trip. "I am super excited, Shirin, that we are finally going to our dream destination. We will go shopping together because there are still a few things to pick up."

Shirin interrupted her sister, saying, "I am not coming with all of you, I have other plans."

Roshani asked after a brief silence, 'What is wrong with you? Where have you been?"

Shirin took a deep breath and said, "I have found my final destination and my true love. Don't ask me to come back, Didi."

Roshani sighed and said, "Why have you altered your plans, my dear sister? Tuli and I intend to go on our anticipated trip to Scotland, and I am confident that you won't pass up this wonderful opportunity for anything else under the sun."

Shirin said boldly, "Didi, I am in a place that is the ideal location for me on Earth." Shirin said with a tranquil and composed expression, "I will take my risk, and I am finally ready to take the final leap of faith. My heart profoundly understands that I am happiest here, among the fields of sunflowers, where life is peaceful and straightforward. Nothing in terms of money or possessions can reverse it."

Roshani said in a serious tone, " It is not easy to let go of all that you have achieved with your hard work in a single moment of hasty decision."

Shirin smiled and said, " I have finally found my true love in Vinay and he is my only true soulmate."

Vinay held Shirin's hand and drew her close. In the warm glow of the setting sun, they sat down on a big rock and Shirin leaned her head on Vinay's shoulders. As they looked together in the direction of the setting sun, the sky changed its hues from bright orange to hot pink giving hope of another new dawn, a new day.

For so long I have wished for this day, a day where our love will find its way.

From my heart deep into your soul our hearts will find the true love-filled way.

Just as a spectacular rainbow emerges on the mountaintop before dissipating into the distance.

One could not tell where it would begin and where it would outdistance.

We must face our fear in accordance with the voice inside.

Take your leap of faith fearlessly; this is how we'll eventually learn to stride.